Passing the Torch

*If World Peace is a castle in the air,
then help put a foundation under it!*

a novel

NENÉ LA ROSA

Passing the Torch: If World Peace is a castle in the air, then help put a foundation under it!

Copyright © 2011 Nené La Rosa. All rights reserved. No part of this book may be reproduced or retransmitted in any form or by any means without the written permission of the publisher.

Published by Wheatmark®
610 East Delano Street, Suite 104
Tucson, Arizona 85705 U.S.A.
www.wheatmark.com

ISBN: 978-1-60494-565-2
LCCN: 2011920679

Who will read my book that I wrote forty years ago, on a manual typewriter, that snarls at the world from the doghouse of discontent?

Winchester, MA 9/1/09

To the memory of my mother, who luckily owned two houses, sold one to send me to school; and to my wife who has nurtured me like a perennial baby.

Sapere Aude. Dare to know.

—Horace

"*The most incomprehensible thing about the universe is that it is comprehensible.*"

—Einstein

The human race without exception had lived and died in a world of illusion, until the last year of the century.

—Arthur Balfour

Passing the Torch

What impact has Armstrong's lunar landing made so far on our world's inhabitants? None. There's no new vision or revision in their point of view. Humanity persists blankly and nonchalantly staring at the sky from the earth, never imagining seeing the Earth from the other extreme end of the Universe millions of miles and light years away. What would humanity see from that commanding perspective? A dense conglomerate of galaxies in which our Milky Way can hardly be detected, our Sun lost in it and our little speck of dust, planet earth, negligible and invisible. Our lack of imagination, together with our individual carapaces limiting our own comprehension beyond ourselves, our day to day preoccupations of earning a living, the frailty of our bodies prone to disease, the unpredictability of our life span, all make us forget about the Universe and our place in it that is astronomically less than zero. And yet, the distant Universe ought to be considered in our defining our destiny. This is critical to the journey toward our becoming truly civilized beings and by accepting that were are infinitesimally small creatures, all of a single species, brothers and sisters living on this speck for as long as it remains habitable, is our only hope of survival.

Tonio and Turri, middle aged professors and culturally orthodox until that point, made the leap and accepted that they were citizens of the earth and abandoned the provincial views of race and national borders. They abandoned the myths and fabulous tenets of the past and looked for new axioms to guide their lives. The conservatives on the faculty clinging to old myths persecuted their two colleagues as mad revolutionaries and inveighed against them that without a creator of the Universe they were rejecting the idea that life on earth had a purpose . They countered: "Who said that the Universe and life have to have a purpose?" Isn't the question of purpose just another man's corollary made out of his anthropomorphism? As soon as primitive man created the flint tool he assumed somebody bigger and stronger than he must have created the fierce environment that surrounded him and placed him in continual peril. He asked for His help. Thus man created the creator as he created the flint tool he used to butcher his prey. The tool had a purpose and so the Big Creator must have created everything for a purpose. The Creator made him and his aids and he began to worship. Tonio and Turri found out how hard it is to remove these illusions from a mankind chained as they are to the rock of ages. Over a century before Tonio and Turri, a poet tried to convert humanity to live in accordance with the new Science, but failed when he wrote: "Man, forget the Achaens, forget their fables; the past is no more. Live in the present reality!" The universe for what we know has no purpose and life has no purpose. Life, whatever its source, is given to us as a gift. Let's live it as an adventure in a favorable environment that we have inherited. Let's create our own purpose! We ought to continue to evolve to a civilized consciousness until we reach World Fraternity and World Peace for all the earth's children. The narrators ask the skeptical reader: If achieving world peace is building castles in the air, then help put foundations under them!

Chapter I

"Wake up world! It's a beautiful spring morning. Step in your gardens and smell the roses! Will you, inhabitants of this planet earth, think to do something new today or will you stick to your old myths, creeds, provincial notion of State, frontiers, prepare for war, research for weapons of mass destruction perfecting your atomic arsenals, polluting a lot more of the earth's biosphere?

Have we all a death wish? It's a beautiful morning, perfect to begin changing lethal ways into beneficial peaceful ones. On this wonderful morning, under a blue, sunny sky made for new beginnings, it's hard for me to go and observe the end of a life.

"Death shouldn't come on sunny days, rather in stormy ones or in dark terrible nights appropriate to tragedy," thought Turri Sicorene, he himself in the winter of his life, entering the hospital where his old friend was clearly near death.

"It's hard for me to go and banter with Tonio in his circumstance, but we will do as we have always done, to the end," he thought bracing himself with a fake nonchalance, facing the imminent death of a precious life. He took the elevator to the fifth floor and entered room 509. There he met Paluzza, Tonio's wife, who was talking to herself while rearranging the two chairs in the room. He greeted Paluzza who took a break and left the room and he went further into the room where Tonio was lying in bed,

"Hello, young man! Still in bed?"

"Who are you? Shouldn't you be in the garden on this beautiful spring morning, rather than visiting a dying old man?" Tonio replied crustily.

"I wish I were. Unfortunately I'm your old student who learned next to nothing from you. I tore myself from my beautiful garden to visit my old teacher and I find that I'm not welcome, and so I'll leave." Turri headed for the door half wondering if his old friend and teacher knew him or not.

"Oh, that's you! You old clown!" said Tonio with a smile.

"Do you esteem me so low as a clown?" Turri retorted pretending to be irritated but glad of a smile and rejoinder.

"I could go even lower than a clown and still not be demeaning you!"

"I don't have to take this abuse," said Turri again heading for the door.

"You're leaving because I didn't recognize

you and took you for a stranger. Is it my fault if I didn't recognize your face and your personality, so indistinctly common?" said Tonio trying a sitting position for a better look at Turri's face .

"I won't let the sting of your words or the stink of your decomposing body kill me. I'll leave now. Good bye," said Turri pretended to be hurt and affronted.

"Oh, please, come back in and sit down! Some time ago I accepted you as one belonging to earth's single species of humankind, and if I failed to recognize you it was because of my poor eyesight. I can't see well or should I say 'good'. I ask you, which is right?" concealing a double meaning.

"If you don't know I won't tell you. Besides, I'm a history teacher, you know."

"What kind of history do you teach? I assume the usual? Full of battles and dates and nothing else? You chose Marathon, Cannae, Zama, Marengo, Yorktown, Bastogne and places of mass slaughter. In other words, you a carnifex inculcating your pupils to become carnifices. Did you call that teaching a moral creed? What else could we expect from you a young man who followed Mussolini. Did you think he was resurrecting the Roman Empire?"

Tonio thought to himself, "I was tainted by the same stupid dream of power and glory and it was a miracle that Turri and I became pacifists and citizens of the world— unfortunately late in life."

"Sir, I was a foolish young man then. At the time empires were everywhere: British, French, Soviet, Japanese, and so why not a restored Roman Empire? When you and I finally became citizens of the world we thought that the notion of empire was gone forever. Now to our dismay it lingers on and still vaguely analyzed while we are in a world economy with a world warming climate. We're still dividing our globe into many nations centuries after Copernicus, Galileo, Newton, and Einstein, and the many great others since have shown us that the earth is not the center. Mankind is only a single species and all of us sons and daughters on this speck of dust. What is the size of our planet that our pride has magnified to the powerful center of the Universe? Nothing really, lost in this infinity. And what is man even in our galaxy? A ridiculous non-entity. And yet our foolish pride make us dream of imperial supremacy over our brothers and sister as if being rulers over them would somehow truly increase our puny status in a Universe that doesn't know our planet exists and if it knew wouldn't care!"

"I must admit that I should have become a world citizen before you. You got there first. I've always taken second place to you although I am your senior and have more brains, am taller and better looking than you." Tonio retorted trying to sound disappointed.

"You are taller than I am, that's all . You were a tall professor short on knowledge," retaliated Turri.

"Asinus asinum fricat, eh? I knew little back then, knowing a lot of people who knew and know less than nothing about everything. Like you, for instance," said Tonio in a derisive way.

"You're a fountain of knowledge except when it comes to knowing how to die silently. Are you afraid of dying?" Turri taunted his friend.

"If I had a choice, I'd choose to live rather than to die," lamented Tonio, now almost in tears.

Turri didn't know how to console the dying man. He had thought keeping up the banter would distract the pain somewhat.

"Remember that our soul will live in heaven and forever in bliss," said Turri although neither of them believed in heaven or in hell. He could tell Tonio was not amused.

"Turri, you don't believe in that nonsense do you?" Paluzza, who had just returned and had been sitting quietly began groaning and left the room again shaking her head.

"No, but Paluzza does. Your wife believes you'll burn forever in hell."

"Hell is the kind of marriage I've made for her and I'm sorry for it. She deserved a better life, poor woman! I was in pursuit of an ideal love and laureled glory. Wisdom came to me too late. Now, getting back to you. You should have run for office. Now you must be 74 or 75, nine years younger than I am. If you can call that young!"

"It's too late now. What would I say if it were not? That mankind is a single species and we all have to cooperate to keep our planet liveable and share it in peace."

"This would have been the message and have made a good speech. I tried to lead you by the hand to it. You didn't go for it even though I tried early enough I think to point out these truths. You had the gift, I didn't, but you gave your rich inheritance away," bemoaned Tonio.

"I thank you, Professor, but that wasn't a political speech. I really do believe in the gospel of world peace and world fraternity, but where are there new apostles? Am I too cynical? As far as I know we're the only two and when you are gone I'll be the only one. Speaking of departure, when is yours? Coming here seems to have shortened my life."

"I'll be gone soon enough, but you, being a fool will live to be one hundred and ten. Fools live longer than wise men do." Tonio joked.

"It's boring arguing with you!" Turri retorted.

"Like old times, eh? We've always argued over things. We couldn't see eye to eye even where we agree, except for once when we both fell in love with the Princess Carlotta Salinas. I wonder what ever happened to her? Do you know?" Tonio said wistfully.

"Do you mean whether she's still alive?" Turri asked.

"I guess she must be long gone. Smart people die early. My sweet dear Paluzza will live forever!" Tonio interjected spying Paluzza once again entering the room.

"There she is now! How can I forget Paluzza? I see her every day."

"I couldn't come to see you without seeing her first," joked Turri.

Annoyed with the comment Tonio interjected, "You're more perceptive than I thought. I bet if you lived to be a thousand you could easily reach an evolved intelligent state."

"Oh, Professor, you're so very kind! And you know what? I don't think I'll be attending your funeral. You're the most stinking, foul mouthed dying old bastard I ever met!" Turri said pacing the room. When he didn't hear any repartee he got close to the bed and realized that his friend had passed out. He grew alarmed.

"Are you listening to me? Are you dead or dozing off? Professor! Wake up!" Turri cried out quickly rubbing his friend's face.

"What? Who's there? Am I in heaven?" Tonio suddenly revived.

"It's me, Turri! You're not in heaven!" he shouted relieved that the old bastard was still alive.

"Oh, I realize that now that I see you there."

"For a second I thought you were dead. ... Not a chance. How long do we have to wait for that event? I mean, one does get tired coming to see a dying old man who never dies. ...Coming here is very expensive, too and has cost me a fortune. Taxi fares went up, too, you know. Professor, give it straight to me, when?" Turri sensed the amusement returning to his teacher's face

"I'll die after I see your beautiful and young wife one last time! She's so young. She's at least ten years younger than you isn't she?"

"Three is more like it."

"Whatever. I still think that you are a very lucky man. You married Ann, the natural daughter of prince Guidelbert Salinas, princess by blood. There is more: you have two children and as far as I know, four grandchildren." Tonio said with envy." I'm lucky, while you old fool have no children!"

"I have Paluzza."

"Lucky her! She fought tooth and nail to have you. I think she regrets the pain and trouble cost her to get you, the most valuable, masculine prize in the world! The stallion with no progeny! She could have done much better."

"And you, are sure you have a progeny? Ann had two children that you call yours. Could be she had them by another man, that athlete, what's his name?"

"You're old and insane! Agatha and Anthony are mine."

"They could have been mine if she didn't tell me that I was not her type."

"She didn't tell you that, you old liar!"

"She did, back then. I can remember things that happened a long time ago but can't remember what I ate an hour ago. When you reach a certain age, you don't live anymore in the present but in the past. You live on memories. I remember when you were sixteen. You were a scoundrel even then! "

"Yes, I was," said Turri. "I almost killed an old man." Turri commented consternated. A big buxom middle-aged nurse came in, went to Tonio's bed, and gave him another dose of morphine.

"Where is Turri?" Tonio Giaccone asked his wife Paluzza, soon after he woke up.

"Turri's gone. You screamed so loudly in your sleep, that he concluded that if you could make such a racket, you had enough energy to last one more day. He left this message for you: Make sure you die tomorrow, because that's the last time he will set foot in this stinking hospital, to visit you, regardless whether you are dead or not."

"Did the s.o.b. really say that?"

"Yes, he did."

"Then I'll die tomorrow, as he wishes. Turri always gets what he wishes. He wanted to marry Ann Nascone, a princess by blood, being the daughter of prince Guidelbert Salinas, natural daughter that is, and he did. Back then, she fell for his lachrymose tale of being a veteran with nobody in the world to take care of him. She went to the town-ramparts, on the second day of his ultimatum, to console in her beautiful arms, the poor orphan boy, pushing thirty then, and agreed to marry him."

"We went to their beautiful wedding."

"Did Turri let the poor girl pay for the wedding and the reception's expenses?"

"Of course not! He paid for everything. He's a go-getter. Soon after their marriage, he bought a beautiful Villa at Fontanelle. We've been at their magnificent home a thousand times. They've two grown children, Agatha and Anthony, and four grand-children while we still live in your parent's house, in need of repair, with a stamp-size yard; and have no children!" Paluzza said with regret.

"You're the St. Francis of Assisi of our time. You gave away your inheritance not to the poor but to the well-off. We have had to live on your meager teacher's salary!" she complained, running to the next room to hide her tears.

"Paluzza, my dear wife, come back here! I'm grateful to you, for having cared for me, all these years. I wish I had kept some of my grandmother's inheritance for your benefit. I should've thought of your future. I'll be gone soon. What will you live on? We've saved very little. Therefore, when I'm gone, don't bury me in a Pyramid!" he bantered, to soothe her thoughts of facing a future of penury.

"I would if I could!"

"A common grave, then. I'll share the same fate of Pericles, Mozart, and other greats."

I'll bury him, Paluzza thought, next to his Archduchess mother, more arrogant than Queen Marie Antoinette. I should have decapitated the pretentious bitch, and let her share the same fate of the queen. When my day comes, I'll leave in my will, to be buried next to my decent parents.

Professor Tonio Giaccone died the next day. The widow called on Turri and Ann for help. They came as soon as possible to hug and comfort their friend in mourning. Paluzza asked Turri to deliver the funeral eulogy. Turri said that it was an honor for him to be asked. Then Paluzza gave him the last papers that Tonio had written before dying. Turri read them and thought their content to be worthy as a eulogy. Tonio had died without finishing what to him seemed the author's synopsis of his life and aspirations. What Turri had to do was to read it at the funeral.

At the right time Turri went to the lectern in the funeral parlor and began to read from professor Tonio Giaccone's manuscript.

"The civilized man lives according to his taste, without impinging on other people's lives. My transition from a bit savage to a bit civilized man, was not that simple. I remember as a boy I searched for the truth, which to me then, was synonymous with God. I wanted to be in contact with the Lord, to walk with him, with his divine hand in mine. I searched for him in deserted chapels, in the still of open fields,and in the expanse of the ocean. My heart's chords thrilled with the harps of Chateaubriand, Scott, Tolstoy, and all the bards who have wept on the banks of solitary lakes,in the echo of chapels' chimes at twilight. Then as a young man I looked within myself, in the expanse of the sky, in the libraries and in the words of the sages. Everywhere I searched I found uncertain talk, and dissatisfied, steeped myself in mysticism. Oh how I longed to see the glory of God, to hear his voice, to be touched even for an instant by his hand and be raised and numbered among those written in the book as a citizen of the New Jerusalem. Oh how many times I prayed to God: Oh Lord, if there is more light in you, increase it in me, make me wiser as the years go by; crown me with the supreme victory of having understood beyond man, beyond the boundaries of the universe, the why of it. I waited to be sent as Amos was sent or Paul or anyone who has proclaimed to have heard the voice of the Lord. While waiting for the blessing of God I followed Paul, participated in his work-and in his sorrows; worked with John in the effort to throw a bridge between heaven and earth, through the Logos made flesh. I supported the charismatic ministry of the Didache; separated with Tertullian, Athens from Jerusalem; sustained Athanasius and homoousion formula. I was tormented with the same spiritual struggle of Augustine and Pascal; full of indignation like Luther, and frustrated like Kierkegaard. I drank out of the same cup which inebriated all those who, through the centuries, have had the supreme desire to see God face to face. I was bestowed many blessings. About the same time, I became an exile. I lost the benefit and consolation of faith. Why? Am I Demas, who forgot Paul for the love of this world? No, certainly not. What was it, that made me change the course of my life, the field of my work; forced me to leave the harbor that had sheltered me from the gales and high seas? Was walking hand in hand with God, not sufficient for me? Could the hope of eternal life so easily bartered for few days of earthly fun? No, certainly not. I had much at stake and lost much. I've changed the course of my life, not for greed and gain, but for the simple reason that what had been true to me, was true no more. I've changed, and yet I still feel the same. I still love ephemeral things emerging from nothingness and vanishing into iridescent clouds; refined sensations provoked by purple sunsets, morning breezes, works of art, rapturous caresses, remembrances of youth, dreams that refuse to die. Carmina non dant panem— and yet I can't get over these worthless trifles. They help smooth the sharp edges of life, as well as the heartaches of sensitive human beings, who have understood more than they can bear. They are nuances that distinguish the refined taste and delicate contours of the best from the rest. Rimbaud, the poet 'maudit' complained: "Il faut s'habiller, se soumettre." He raised a very good question, which can be answered according to our individual grade of absorption and mastering of the many aspects of our culture. If your disposition and taste urge you to go naked, and you see it as a personal fulfilment, by all means, if it does not hurt anyone else, do it! On the other hand, there are those who relish rituals and paraphernalia of our culture, and others who go beyond them, and find relief and joy in what, to the uninitiated, seem trifles and frills, that can be disposed of without altering the style and course of life. Lately, these same things have been held in such disrepute, that only the feeble-minded bother with them; so much so that, when I was an adolescent, I often asked my mother whether I was stupid, given my inclination for these disreputable trifles, while I was groaning under scientific subjects, differential equations, imaginary numbers, and the like. She used to comfort me, saying that I was at least average, and in her expansive moods, in her mother's eye, a genius. I had to wait till a sage opened fully my eyes, to see clearly how things stood topsy-turvy and showed me that nature, sunsets, etc. were fields of excellence, while Calculus, Medicine, Physics etc., were ancillary, marginal fields that the average intelligent person can deal with, by opaquing 90 percent of his intellect. I did just that and easily built my own computer on the simple Leibnizian binaries, mastered differential equations, rent the veil of atomic secrets. Then the statement by Oppenheimer, that the work of Einstein could only be accomplished by a simple mind, made sense to me. The place Ortega y Gasset relegated the scientists was probably the right one, while in Proust's eyes they belonged to the Douzieme Arrondissement, and their precedence in court to the 119th place. They are the new artisans, with their eyes fixed to the phenomenon before them, without the benefit of seeing antecedents and consequents to it, like pictures in caves without a back-ground. They are irresponsible children playing with matches, that at any moment, may start a conflagration. They don't sit at the ample table of civilization, rather, under the table, feeding on crumbs and leftovers. Left to themselves they have hastened a barbarian age, unequalled in history. One of these enfants terribles, with grey hair, but perennial children, complained that having contributed to life with his work, life, ungratefully was leaving him and in torment besides. He simply mistook and equated the labors of his occupation, at the service of the state and in the effort of war as if they aimed at life's improvement rather than destruction and death. We can see that excellent scientists don't necessarily make good men, they make almost always, bad thinkers. By using their interdependence on business and state, they have been able to peter out the most exquisite streams of culture as expendable and unnecessary, thus adding more weight, to the already heavy fetters that chain mankind. The results of the electronic revolution are: The discarding of refined intuitions, the neglect of comprehensive syntheses, and the accession to the throne of myopic science, i.e., the atrophy of total intelligence. The Bolshevic revolution accomplished the same thing. It not only killed the nobility, but also intelligent people. Had there been left any intelligent Russian, they could have check-mated the United States of America, by making Canada and Mexico nuclear powers. Instead they squandered their energies, helping petty and sundry little nations in the wrong places. Meantime China and India are rising as world powers. As soon as they join the atomic-bomb club and achieve the electronic stage, they will flex their muscles, believing in the idiocy of becoming the sole world empire. That's the great illusion of less than mediocre minds, also very sick. They can not see that slavery is gone and with it the empires on which they rested. Supremacy over others, always the cause of war, is also gone. And yet, persons with sick minds still wage war on weak, small nations, to quench their thirst for human blood. Those insane persons, cannibals indeed, shouldn't be at the head of large and powerful nations, rather kept in insane institutions. Let's hope that things get better in the near future. In the meantime I enjoy myself with my frills, always longing for a place where I could share them with like minded people. But where is that Shangri-La? Are there in the entire world, enough decent human beings to establish a colony of real civilized people? I would pay any price to be in their company, so that I could read in their hearts and they in mine. It's a shame that the entire world population hasn't reached yet that level of civilization! Turri and I carry the Torch to accomplish that sublime goal.

   I stopped writing, being interrupted by my

friend and colleague Turri Sicorene who had come to take me in my tiny yard and to marvel at a new thing in the night sky. I went out and saw, at a first impression, a falling star that wasn't falling. Turri, standing next to me, told me it was Sputnik, a satellite put in space by the Russians. I hadn't looked at the night sky since I was a boy and now I was looking at the starry sky and to this man made star. In a few minutes it was gone but I kept staring at the myriads of stars that filled every inch of the sky above me. This new wonder should have made me feeling bigger as a human being for this mankind great accomplishment, instead I felt diminished by realizing that I lived in this speck of dust called planet earth,an infinitesimal part of the immense universe, full of galaxies that overwhelmed my perception and my imagination. Turri was likewise struck by the reality that we, now professors at the University, had inculcated in our students, I, mostly ancient Greek culture, anchored in the Aegean sea, and Turri teaching who had done what in the same corner of the world. We not only had relegated ourselves in that parcel of land and culture but hadn't really thought of the immense universe that dwarfed our insignificant planet with its trillions of stars larger than our sun. When Neil Armstrong landed on the moon and made available to us the picture of our earth taken from there, it made clear to all of us in this planet that we are lost in a vast universe and that we'd better take care of it, and stick together to preserve it. As a perceptive poet admonished us:

Forget the fables, forget the Achaeans, and go buy an affordable telescope! And what have we done with the new knowledge of our place in the universe? Next to nothing. Have we, inhabitants of our speck of dust planet, got together as perhaps the only precarious sprout of life in the whole universe and care for one another as brothers? No. We continue to fight one another as we did in the past and died as enemies, forgetting that we all survive or perish either by our own doing by polluting it to make it unable to support lifelike the moon where not a blade of grass grows and life is impossible there. Turri's younger than I am, but as usual, perceived the consequences of Sputnik and Armstrong landing on the moon before I did,that the axioms our culture stood on were made obsolete by the new knowledge. Turri, as usual, began preaching the gospel of the new reality before I did. The two of us have since spread the word that mankind being one species living in this speck of dust lost in an immense universe, has to make it a world of fraternity and peace to survive. After all these years we haven't converted many, because most of our fellow inhabitants of mother earth still cling to the old axioms as eternal truths rather than perceptions of a past knowledge, appropriate to those times. The effect of this resistance to the new reality is the nonchalant attitude of multitudes advancing toward the abyss ahead. The status quo ante remaining the same we still have wars with loss of lives, habitat, and infrastructure. The civilian survivors are left without a roof above their heads, without food,water, sewer, health care and the other amenities of any sort. In other words: without a life worth living. That's a shame! It seems that Turri and I have put our message in a bottle, let it float on the ocean and it hasn't reached any shore. Perhaps we have converted to world fraternity and world peace one of our old pupils by the name 'Nene.' Alas, he emigrated to the U.S.A. Will he be successful spreading the new gospel of peace in America? Now and then he comes to see us but the news he brings us is dismal. And yet Turri and I don't despair. Ladies and gentlemen, Professor Tonio Giaccone's synopsis ends here. I know that this is not the right place and time to propagate his and mine gospel of world peace, but I ask anyways is here among you gentlemen and ladies, anyone who would raise his or her hand,to volunteer taking the Torch of World Fraternity and carry it forward toward its sublime goal? I don't see any raised hands and no volunteers."

"What about your son and daughter?"

"They are here and don't volunteer either! That's a good question. My son Anthony is one of the herd. He chose archeology and is embedded in the past rather than exploring the future. Even at the beginning of our mission he thought that Tonio and I were wasting our time like new Don Quixotes charging windmills. My daughter Agatha takes care of four young children and has no time for anything else. I ask your pardon for this digression.

Let's return to Professor Tonio Giaccone. He was a good man. We know that people are born, live, decay, and then vanish from this earth. I hope that professor Tonio Giaccone will be remembered for a long time!

After everybody there was gone, Ann and Turri went to embrace the widow Paluzza. This kind of warm embrace Antoine de Saint Exupery called the real human charity, worth infinitely more than money, flowers or condolence cards. Ann and Turri did more than embrace Paluzza, they took her to live with them.

Professor Turri Sicorene died eight years after his friend Tonio's death.

Tonio Giaccone and Turri Sicorene were my teachers, when I was an adolescent in Sicily. We remained friends even after I emigrated to the U.S.A. They didn't accomplish any feat to make them famous, except what one of their pupils, on our twentieth class reunion, praised them, that we entered their classrooms boys and came out men. They and I grew up in the twentieth century, full of human bloodshed, fratricidal wars, revolutions, precision bombs, and ultimately atom bombs. The twentieth century will also be notoriously known for having polluted our rivers, lakes, seas, oceans, the air we breath, and the biosphere that makes life on earth possible. Will the twenty first century reclaim what the last century polluted or add to it, and make our planet earth desolate like the moon, where not a blade of grass grows? I'm an optimist, and hope for a better future, without fratricidal wars and a liveable earth for us all. Those teachers of mine didn't increase much my knowledge of civilization, only pointed to me to try to contribute my little block to the unfinished building of civilization. Why did I bother, to write a synopsis of their, provincial lives? Because they remained my friends for life. Turri Sicorene I loved in particular because he implanted in me the vision of a global peace, and a global fraternity. I'm grateful to him for this flame he lit in me, that made me a somewhat civilized human being.

"Tomorrow morning I'm expected at Villa Augusta. Did you hear that?" Turri asked his mother while she was running about from room to room doing her chores.

"I heard you. I am old but not completely deaf

as you think," she answered him when she came back into the living-room with a duster in her hand.

"Mom, you know what I mean. Don't make a federal case out of this. Anyway, Princess Carlotta Salinas asked me there to thank me for a service I rendered her, Isn't it wonderful!" he exclaimed in a joyful mood.

"It's wonderful as you said, and I am glad for you. I knew something good would befall us since Easter when, in the Cathedral, the curtain fell straight without the least incident. The saying goes that when the curtain parts and shows the resurrected Jesus without incidents it's a sign of good luck to all who attend," she mused. Gemma however was apprehensive, on the one hand she was glad for her son's new found happiness. Lately, he had been despondent, suffering from a sentimental disappointment, she had guessed that common teenagers' calamity. Turri rarely went out, spending a lot of time indoors in the dark, sitting in bed, and wasting his youth away. Then, to her relief, he ventured out again. And now this wonderful mood of his was a welcomed event. On the other hand, Gemma feared that Turri's happiness would be short-lived.

She stopped dusting the cheap pine furniture and went to sit next to Turri on the old sofa, she had herself re-upholstered in green damask. She wanted to warn her son of the great disillusionment he was exposing himself to in courting a princess. She could tell that Turri was so deeply infatuated with Princess Carlotta Salinas that he had entirely overlooked the stakes against him.

"Son, can I try to put some common sense into this hubbard squash brain of yours?" she asked pointing to his head, in an affectionate banter.

"Mom, I'm sorry but don't try to dissuade me this time. Squashheads have no salt in them but they fall in love like anybody else."

"In your state you think you can walk on water, but can you?"

Turri brushed aside her warnings as unnecessary flukes. He kissed her and went to bed but slept little and badly. It was worse for him than an exam's vigil night. In the morning he had to make a good impression on Princess Carlotta at any cost. He got up at seven o'clock. Before taking a shower he asked his mother to get him his light brown gabardine suit a white shirt, a not-too-gory necktie, brown shoes, etc.

"For a boy you're too preoccupied with the impression you will make on Princess Carlotta Salinas!" Gemma told her son. "Don't forget that she is twice your age and has also played all sorts of tricks with men long before you were born."

"Mom, the princess is only twenty-four years old!" Turri shouted angrily at his mother.

Only twenty-four years old while you'll be eighteen next Saturday and you believe you're a man of the world already! Go wash yourself behind your earlobes, my child!"

"Mom, thanks for your vote of confidence, and your moral support you're giving me.

"I am only trying to open your eyes to reality."

"Mom, you don't believe in spontaneous love which like a wild flower blossoms wherever nobody suspects it would?"

"Yes, I do. It's rare and ephemeral, though."

Turri realized that arguing with his mother was a waste of time and of effort.

"She has a few good points, I have to admit," Turri commented to himself while trying to make a knot with that rebellious piece of cloth called necktie. "If I were at least twenty years old. If I were rich. If I were somebody, I'd have a better chance to win her over. What can I do? Destiny has dictated that I take my chance to win her love prematurely. So be it!"

Turri finished putting his clothes on. He spent a long time in front of the mirror. He dissolved into his chestnut haircut long, a dab of pomade Linetti and combed it back into a "fishbone," the style in vogue. He hadn't worked at his part-time job at the counter of the drugstore on the corner of Seas and Mille Streets for a while and was broke. He needed the money to buy six roses and pay the taxi-cab fare. He was mortified to have to ask his mother for five lire. She went into her bedroom to fetch the money. On other occasions like this when he had asked her to give him five lire she had given him ten. Not this time.

"This is wasted money," she told Turri putting the five-lire bill in his hand.

"She still thinks it's stupid of me to dare courting Princess Carlotta. She doesn't know what a burning flame Carlotta has kindled inside of me and that it's destroying me. I must try quenching this thirst I have for her love rather than doing nothing and letting it turn me into ashes."

"Poor as I am," Gemma tried to comfort him, "I'd give you five hundred lire or all I have to my name if it would buy your happiness, my son. Unfortunately for us the princess deals in millions." She stared at him. Her boy had grown. He was a young man ready to plunge into the torrid waters of a profligate princess' love. She hugged him.

"What an irresistible lover you have become! Still you look your age. Shouldn't I make you a mustache with a black crayon to let you appear more mature?" she teased him.

"Mom, a fake mustache is not going to help. Why didn't you conceive me three or four years earlier? That would have been a great help. Anyway, things being as they are I'll do my best to win princess Carlotta's love. Fortune often favors those who dare and I dare to the utmost."

"My God, my boy is not ready to plunge into the world. He hasn't grown enough to avoid being hurt. He'll touch the hot stove again as he did when he was very small," Gemma thought alarmed. Soon the tooting horn of the taxi-cab was heard.

"The taxicab's arrived. I have to go. Arivederci, mother." Turri kissed Gemma and dashed out of the house and into the cab. The taxi sped Northbound toward Villa Augusta. At the wheel of the black and red striped Fiat 1100 was a fat, dark skinned young man who kept morosely quiet. Turri wasn't in a talkative mood also. He had his heart and mind in turmoil.

"Suppose she likes me, what shall I do?" he questioned himself. "I am inexperienced. I can't pretend. I'll play it by ear," he concluded.

In the meantime the taxi had entered Villa Augusta's wrought-iron gate and was approaching the main building through the long, palm flanked driveway. The cab stopped in front of the perron to the main entrance. Turri alighted, paid the fare and stared at the imposing structure before him.

"Late Baroque," he commented. "It's a befitting dwelling for a princess." He mounted the shiny marble steps that led to the entrance. At that very moment a butler in light-gray attire appeared on the threshold. Turri introduced himself.

"I am Signor Turri Sicorene."

The butler did a slight bow. Turri added, "I have come to call on Princess Carlotta Salinas."

"Signor Sicorene, the princess will be notified of your arrival. Follow me, please." The butler was in his sixties, tall, with rare traces of having been blond haired once. He was as stiff as a board and as pretentious as all imbeciles. Turri followed the butler making faces at him behind his back. He took another look at the gardens from the open windows on the first floor corridor. He saw many exotic and domestic trees, and flowers and not one fig tree "Biffari." He didn't recognize most of the plants.

"I must take a course in botany," he commented.

Turri followed Gaston. He had named the butler Gaston as all the butlers he had seen in the movies were named Gaston. While crossing corridors, halls, and salons, all decorated and furnished in rococo period, glittering with myriads of mirrors and crystal chandeliers, Gaston probed into Turri.

"Signor Sicorene, do you live at Palermo?" he inquired.

"No. I'm from Cuntuvi." Turri replied.

"A very old Carthaginian town," Gaston commented in a derogatory way.

"You're full of knowledge and a bit of venom," Turri replied vexed.

"I didn't mean to imply that. Are you a friend of Prince Philip Salinas, Princess Carlotta's younger brother? He's a couple of years older than you."

"No, but I wish I were."

"You wouldn't have been the first plebeian the reckless young prince soils his rank and name by associating with."

"Why are you insulting me? I'll be famous and rich someday. Remember my words!"

Isn't it what every poor devil hopes for and dreams about? You'll die as penniless and nameless as you're now."

"The future will tell."

"Your future will be as bleak as your past. Has any member of your family ever been distinguished in any field, besides that of crime that is?"

"Aren't you a little nosy? And do you ask the other guests these questions or am I the exception?" Turri irritably rebuked the butler.

"Please don't be angry with me, Signor Sicorene. It's part of my duty. You, being from the low middle-class, how did you happen to meet Princess Carlotta Salinas?"

"I should punch him in the nose," Turri

thought, but for Carlotta's sake I'll oblige answering his, impudent questions."

"I'm low middle-class as you guessed. My father was a civil engineer. I don't remember him well. He died when I was still an infant. He was not a saint. He was a gambler, a womanizer, and a champion pool player. He won a lot of money and squandered all of it. He left enough money for a college education for me, and my mother a small pension. Shouldn't I make this confession to Princess Carlotta rather than to you?"

"You're a sensible young man, why did you come here I wonder?"

"I told you I was invited by the princess and here I am. Certainly the Princess and I are worlds apart. I belong to the 'Biffari' side of society."

"I don't know what you mean by that."

"You're not Sicilian are you, Gaston?"

"No. I'm from Piedmont."

"It figures. Anyway in this island the middle class, both in their town houses and in their summer cottages always have a fig-tree called "Biffari" in their backyards. Here I haven't seen any.

A definite sign that this is aristocratic soil."

"I see, but you're digressing prolixly from the point."

"Gaston, you have knowledge, you're honest, and I have to add, you have an excellent vocabulary. Now back to the point. We have walked the equivalent of half a kilometer. How much more to the princess?"

"A couple of more corridors."

"Then I'll have to tell you how I know Princess Carlotta in a synopsis. I saw her for the first time a couple of years ago in the foyer of the Teatro Massimo at Palermo. She was escorted by the late Prince Giovanni Alliata."

"Did you meet the prince, also?" Gaston asked astonished.

"I didn't say I met the princess and the prince. I said I saw them together. I was fifteen years old and I was going to the Teatro Massimo for the first time. I had a ticket for the performance of the Aida in my pocket. Because I love pageantry, therefore I lingered in the foyer, watching the aristocrats and the financiers come with their bejeweled chic ladies in chauffeured limousines. It was in that foyer that I saw Princess Carlotta Salinas escorted by prince Giovanni Alliata coming out from a purple sunset.

"Ah! If I were a prince. If I were at least twenty years old, I'd wrest her from him," I said to myself. I had never seen a woman so charming, classy, and beautiful before. Think of it I have not seen any like her after that either. Anyway, there she was so close to me that I got her perfume in my nostrils. She wore a white decollete and an ermine fur cape. She was slender and petite but what an harmonious sensuous body! I was staring at her and hadn't noticed I was keeping the prince away from her. In the prince's opinion I wasn't any competition and he magnanimously smiled at me. We both knew what a great catch he had made. Soon they went to their box and I to my humble third balcony seat, from where the stage appeared no larger than a postage stamp and the singers were colorful specks of dust. I missed most of the Opera. I was trying to watch the princess most of the time. I missed the end also because the prince and the princess left long before the final curtain came down. I rushed to see her departure. I missed it. From up near the dome where I was sitting it takes a long time to come down the stairs to the ground floor. By the time I was out in Piazza Verdi, the princess and the prince were gone. Since that evening I have compared every girl I have met with the princess and all of them have fallen way below her in every way. In other words, once I saw Princess Salinas my eyes have been open to beauty, class, and distinction to such an excellence that I couldn't ever settle for less. You might say, how could they keep me on a farm after I had seen Paree!"

"Signor Sicorene. You're digressing again."

"Sorry, Gaston. I'll get to how I met Princess Carlotta very soon. You have to understand that I couldn't fall in love with any other girl. In these two years I settled for second best once and what a disappointment it was to me!"

"Are you getting to the point?"

"I'm very close to it. You see I used to go to this rocky solitary beach to the Northwest. Northwest from my house, that is. Have you been there?"

"No. I haven't."

"Which proves that you are full of knowledge area honest, have an excellent vocabulary, and also are careful. So careful that you haven't been there. I don't blame you. The cliffs are so sharp that if you are careless they will cut off your feet."

"You're careful I suppose."

"Yes, I usually am. That day, however I was careful with my feet but careless with my heart. I let this bitch, if you pardon my French, make a fool of me. She married this old bastard about your age, and senile like you, and I almost killed myself for her. The wound healed a little at a time. I haven't gone back to that beach since. Instead I began to visit this sandy beach on the Southeast."

"Southeast from your house, that is."

"Touche! Gaston, you're sharp and have a good memory. Usually people your age are senile, but you're razor sharp."

"Let's not linger on compliments, please."

"As you wish. Anyway the beach is called, at low tide as you can walk for miles on sand and meet very few people there."

"You son of a gun you went there on purpose. You knew that Prince Giovanni Alliata had been killed at Amba Alagi in the Abyssinian war, and you played your card with Princess Carlotta. You knew that she used to ride at vespers on that beach, and you went there to see and there to be seen by her!" Gaston said angrily.

"Gaston, hold your horses! When I saw her there for the first time I didn't know of her habit. Therefore I was surprised when I saw her on that black stallion passing by me. God, how beautiful she was! Of course I went back to the Viscione beach the next day at vespers to see if she would ride there again as a matter of a habit or if the time I saw her it was only by chance her first and last time. I waited. When the sky began to turn red I saw the princess appear from a distance on that black stallion. Seeing her again was a stroke of luck for me. She filled my heart with joy. Now that I knew she would come at the Viscione every day at vespers, I went there every vesper to get a glimpse of her beauty. My heart wanted a lot more from her, but seeing the princess was better for me than simply dreaming of her."

"Did you have to let her fall from the horse in order to get your dirty little hands on her, you criminal? You could have gotten her badly hurt."

"Gaston, you've got it all wrong. I wouldn't hurt the princess for all the gold in the world.

It was an accident. You know how stupid horses are. Her beautiful stallion is no exception. He saw that her beautiful stallion because he saw a piece of paper fluttering in the breeze, reared and threw the princess. I was so mad at that stupid horse that I wanted to kill him with my own hands. I was afraid that she had been hurt more than you can think. I love her, don't you understand that, you pinhead? She fell head on and soon was turning blue. I rushed to help her. I didn't know what to do. I must have given her mouth to mouth resuscitation. Anyway she wasn't badly hurt, thank God. When she regained consciousness she thanked me for having helped her. I also went to fetch her horse and she thanked me again. She got back on the horse, and before leaving she asked me, "Can I ask you what your name is, sir?"

"It's an honor for me to tell you, Princess Salinas. I'm Turri Sicorene, and I have always been at your service, your highness."

"Not as a servant as you protest to be, but as a friend, come tomorrow morning at ten o'clock at Villa Augusta to see me, please." "I'll be there, Princess," I answered as happy as a beggar being elevated to the purple, and this morning here I am in this magnificent villa. Is this a villa, a palace, a castle, or what?"

"A palace I should say."

"To me it's a castle. Like the castles in the

fairy-tales, where princesses usually live. We have castles in Cuntuvi, you should know."

"How many castles are there? I thought there was only one."

"You're right, and besides a good part of it was demolished. The mote was filled with dirt, and no barons live there anymore. Under its roof it shelters criminals now."

"Criminals?"

"It has been converted into a prison."

"I see. If you don't behave discreetly with the princess you will wind up in that castle yourself. Prince Guidelbert Salinas will see to it."

"Gaston, you're cruel. I thought we had become friends, and I see we haven't."

"So you have come here to get your reward. How much do you want for having helped the princess when she fell from her horse?"

"I didn't come here to get my reward in money or otherwise. I was invited by the princess to be her guest. Therefore lead me to her please!"

They walked in silence. At the end of a long corridor they reached a spacious veranda with a carved-stone balustrade and a pensile garden.

"Wait here please, while I see whether the Princess will receive you." Gaston told Turri. Turri saw the butler disappear behind dwarf palm trees shrubs, and exotic fruit-trees.

"Just like in Versailles in the old days as I've

read," Turri commented. "Besides the real gardens the aristocrats need the pensile ones."

Gaston soon came back and told Turri, "Carlotta Maria, Adeburgos-Vandimir Princess of Salt will receive you. Please. Now follow me, Signor Turri Sicorene."

"Cut out all that crap you old fool!" Turri almost shouted at Gaston's out of place formality. He followed the butler through a meander of shrubs and what not, and suddenly he was standing before Princess Carlotta. She was lying on a chaise lounge, wearing a revealing yellow colored chiffon sundress. She greeted her guest and welcomed him with a friendly smile. Turri bowed and kissed the soft hand she held out for him. If Gaston hadn't been there Turri would have had the audacity to kiss her lips. The princess entreated him to sit next to her in a wicker chair.

"Signor Sicorene, I am sorry to receive you here and so informally. It's because of the torrid weather. It seems that today it will be unbearable," she said apologetically.

"You may leave!" she told Gaston. "Marina has made ready the refreshments Signor Sicorene and I will need."

Gaston was reluctant to leave.

"Get lost!" Turri felt like shouting at the butler. Gaston left shaking his head.

"Princess Carlotta's making a big mistake receiving a fresh boy like Turri. Seeing her almost naked as she is, he might get ideas into his stupid little head about getting intimate with the princess, and I won't be present to break every bone in his body and throw what's left to the hounds," ruminated Gaston. What will prince Salinas say when he finds out I let a boy from the Striscia get near his daughter? He'll blow his top and I'll be the scapegoat. It's all her fault. On the other hand, the poor girl might have a loose screw in her head as a result of her fall from the horse. However, I blame myself for having let the boy in. What can I do now? If he dares to touch the princess, even with one of his little dirty fingers, I am going to chop his head off," ruminated Gaston.

"Princess, how are you this morning?" Turri inquired earnestly as soon the butler left. "I hope you don't suffer from any ill effects from the fall."

"Signor Sicorene, how kind of you to inquire about my health," she answered him pleased.

"Last evening I called Doctor Galfano and he found I suffered a slight concussion. He gave me the proper medication and I feel in a small degree below normal."

"In that case I'll leave right away. It would be unwise of me to stay and tax your convalescent state," Turri told her apologetically.

"No, don't leave, please," the princess entreated. "I thank you for your concern about my wellbeing, but your company will help my recovery," she reassured Turri. "Please come and sit a little closer to me!"

Turri didn't need much coaxing to do that and got closer to her to become inebriated by her scent. Carlotta stared at Turri and her eyes saw him in a double image. One was that of a young man called Turri Sicorene, unknown to her, and of whom she couldn't have cared less. The other was the image of her late betrothed Giovanni Alliata whom she had loved and whose memory she still cherished.

"I keep seeing Giovanni's resemblance in every young man I meet, although in fact there might be none whatsoever. I'm nuts. I should see a shrink," she was ruminating. She stared at Turri in an effort to see things straight.

"God, the resemblance between this young man and Giovanni is real," she had to admit. "Not only does he look like Giovanni at seventeen-eighteen, but also he has his precise swaggering. No wonder I fell in love with Turri the first time I saw him at the Viscione beach," she commented to herself while pulling the bodice of her sundress up.

"I should have put on something else," she said to herself. "What I am wearing is so revealing, and also if I don't pull it up continuously it will slide down and expose my bust."

The worst was yet to come. At the first attempt she made to roll onto her side, a flap of her sundress got caught under her body while the other flap snapped open and rolled out lengthwise. It exposed her entire body to the astonished look of Turri. He glanced at her charms and decently looked away. Carlotta quickly covered herself, red with embarrassment.

Voila, the secret's out. Revelation right in the beginning. Did I do that on purpose although unconsciously?" she asked herself.

Turri may take it to mean that I don't want to waste any time in seducing him, although I don't feel up to it. Anyway he's ready. I can feel that from his heavy breathing and his dry throat."

Carlotta tried to cool down their emotions with two glasses of iced tea, knowing well that two icebergs- couldn't have accomplished that task. She knew of being at the mercy of a passion whose vortex sooner or later she wouldn't be able to escape, but not today. No sooner had she finished drinking her tea than she felt a bout of dizziness come over her. Her stomach began to turn as it had done the night before.

"My God, don't let me puke here in front of my guest!" she prayed. "If things get worse I won't have time to reach the nearest bathroom down the corridor. What shall I do? Shouldn't I dismiss Turri right away or is it too late?"

Before she could find a solution her dizziness grew worse and her nausea reached the breaking point. Ghostly pale she got up from the chaise lounge and barely made it to the balustrade, leaned out of it and began puking.

"God, I feel so ashamed!" was the last thought that troubled her mind before she passed out. She would have hit the hard mosaic floor if Turri hadn't rushed to catch her in his arms and prevent it.

"What shall I do?" he asked himself confused, with that precious load in his trust. He shouted for help but nobody was nearby to hear or see him. Turri in a hurry carried Carlotta to the first bedroom he saw in the corridor and laid her body onto bed. No signs of life were coming from her inert body, now as cold as ice. He saw a vial of perfume on the dressing bureau, reached for it and let her inhale it. She didn't react to it. I am a jerk. I don't know how to help the woman I love, when she desperately needs it!" He blamed himself. Turri was now deeply worried as Carlotta's body remained icy cold. He began to massage her limbs and here and there over her body where he thought it could help, trying to make her regain consciousness.

"My God, don't let her die!" he prayed in tears. "Princess, wake up! I love you! I love you!" he cried while she remained still and icy. "How shall

I warm her up?" he thought again. She was lying on top of the bed covers. Turri pulled the covers over her. The best way to warm her up was to lay next to her. He did that and began to hug her, to caress her. Seconds went by which to him seemed hours. She was getting a bit warm. Soon she began to regain consciousness and he jumped out of bed, hoping she hadn't noticed he had been in bed with her. However, he was jubilant. "I thank you, Lord, for having spared her! Put it on my account!" he prayed.

The princess opened her blue eyes and it didn't take her long to regain her bearings. She didn't know exactly what had followed after she fainted, but she surmised what had taken place. She took Turri's hand in hers still cold. "I thank you, my new friend, for the care you have given me," she told him deeply moved. "Without your help I might have gotten hurt. Not only that, you also carried me here helped me regain consciousness, and also you prayed for me. I heard you praying while I was in a dreamlike state."

"Holy smoke! If she knows these things, she also might know that I lay in bed with her, hugged caressed, and massaged her. What will she think of my behavior? Will she believe I did that purely for the purpose of warming her up? I hope she didn't notice what I myself didn't know I was doing in the fervor of the moment." Unfortunately for Turri, Carlotta had a vague idea of what had actually happened.

"I needed heat and you kindly supplied it to me," she added, showing a bit of resentment in her tone.

"It was thoughtless of me, princess, I didn't know what I was doing," he said apologetically and blushing crimson.

"She's right to bring it up and chastise me for it," he agreed.

However he was mistaken on this point. Princess Carlotta was indeed disgusted, but not with him, rather with herself and with the turn of the events. She was furiously disappointed that they had ended up in the same bed so soon, and without her approval. Deep down in her being she longed to give herself to Turri but she was cross at the circumstances which had taken the initiative away from her. She was a domineering type who wanted control over the events that touched her life. She tried to retain her power to mold them at will, although she felt so weak. While her head was still aching and her entire body was in need of rest, she knew she couldn't afford the fatigue and joy of love making. Her only way to regain her lost initiative on the matter was to tell Turri frankly how deeply she cared for him. "From his side of the bargain, he isn't bidding for unseen goods," she ruminated.

"He had the opportunity of his life to weigh, inspect, and touch me; therefore he knows how and what I'm made of." Carlotta thought as she lifted her head a bit from the pillow. "

"Turri, come near me," she called tenderly. "Will it come as a surprise to you to know that I fell in love with you the first time I set sight on you?" she confessed unashamedly. Turri no sooner heard her words than he rushed into her arms and kissed her lips that he had dreamed and longed for for so long a time, then he answered her question.

"It's a blessed surprise, Princess, but I have hoped with all my soul and for ages and ages that you would love me."

"Does it mean that you love me?" she asked teasingly.

"If I were wise," he answered holding her to his bosom, "I'd be cautious and keep it a secret what I feel for you, thus I'd avoid being exposed to ridicule. Common sense exhorts me to suppress this mad feeling which is driving me crazy and refuses to see the many obstacles that block the way to its fulfillment. Just the same the fact remains that I am madly in love with you, princess Carlotta Salinas. I dare revealing what I feel for you because keeping it a secret is to me more painful than all the laughs and abuses I'll certainly get from you, and every body else for having set sight so far above my state."

Carlotta was inebriated by Turri's declaration of love, pure and turbulent, as new as a dawn of day, and as old as the invention of this kind of love in our civilization. She hugged him as strongly as her weak strength permitted her.

"My love, we are in deep trouble," she whispered to him."How shall we protect our impossible love from the envious forces of the world?"

No sooner had she spoken those words than she regretted having uttered them.

"This is sheer madness! What's happening to me? Am I gone nuts? Can the rainbow be reached and grasped? He's a boy and yet can grasp that this is a folly. It seems that I am trying to give my mind a sabbatical, escaping from logic, time, responsibilities, civil and moral restraints. I am ready to plunge into an ephemeral fling of pure hedonism in a vacuum, insulated from the reality of the world. It's only a fling that to-morrow will be gone and forgotten, keep telling myself. Will the boy recognize, its ephemeral quality or will he take it as everlasting love and be hurt when summer's over and we will have to part forever,going back to our two different worlds? It's better to kill this passion in the bud, thus I'll deprive myself of a certain amount of pleasure but I will also spare him from getting hurt," Carlotta was reasoning while holding Turri unto her bosom.

Evidently reason has little leverage over passion because while she was thinking of suppressing the latter she let Turri get deeper into it by not stopping him. "How does one stop what's so marvelously pleasant?" she asked herself. Turri, on the other hand, was so madly happy holding Carlotta in his arms that he forgot the world and its harsh realities. He was inebriated by her scent; ecstatic by the contact with her silky skin, tenderly suffocated within her breasts. Under the spell of a mild form of delirium he was now kissing every part of her body trying to explore further into her, below the surface, in the mysterious abyss where the beginning of life and of love dwell. Carlotta stopped him.

"Turri, my love, not now. I'm still weak and so tired. Go home and come back tonight at ten," she told him tenderly. Turri obeyed her and reluctantly released her from his embrace. "I'll feel better by then," she added. Turri sat on the bed near Carlotta visibly disconsolate. "You're impatient, aren't you?" she rebuked him teasingly. "I am asking you to wait ten hours not ten months. Come kiss me, and then go!'

Turri went to her, kissed her lips and then headed for the door. He rushed back to Carlotta. "How shall I come back? Will the Princess instruct Gaston to let me in tonight?" he asked Carlotta anxiously.

"Of course not," she mischievously answered him.

"Princess, if you won't instruct the servants to let me in tonight, does it mean you're trying to get rid of me in a polite way?" Turri asked Carlotta sadly.

"I am not trying to get rid of you," she assured him. "I want you back here tonight, but you are going to use the garden door near the South entrance. Try not to be seen by anyone. It will be easy to do so in the darkness of the night. Can you do that? "

"Yes, I can, Princess," Turri answered bravely.

"It's all set then. And do me a favor, from now on stop calling me Princess. Call me Carlotta."

"As you wish, Carlotta."

"You learn fast. Go now. I'll see you at ten."

"There is one thing I have to know. Will the garden door be open then?"

"No, but you will have the key in your pocket."

"How?"

"You'll find the key in the gardener's brown coat hanging in the wardrobe on the veranda. The wardrobe is a few feet away from my chaise-lounge. Before leaving, go to the veranda and get the key. It's the old gardener's. Use it tonight. I'll be waiting for you at the end of the path that leads to the back-stairs. Go now. I'll see you tonight!"

"I'll do every thing the way you told me. I'll be here tonight at ten, my love." Turri kissed Carlotta's soft white, long-fingered hand and left the room. He went to the veranda, got the key to the gate of heaven, and left Villa Augusta walking on air.

Chapter II

Tonio irritably opened the green glass-paneled door and dashed out of the house. He didn't slam it as his mood suggested to him. Instead he closed it gently. Tonio was exasperated with his mother, but since he was a little boy it had been inculcated in him, sometimes with kindness and at times with a rap on the head, never to slam doors in general, and not this one in particular. Tonio crossed the narrow walk that ran between the two flower beds of the front yard.

"How an intelligent and educated woman like my mother can believe in so many superstitions is beyond me," he grumbled. Moreover, she asked me, a full grown man of twenty-four, and a professor, to go and consult the Sibyl. I can't and I'll never do such a stupid thing."

He opened the gate of the high stone fence which enclosed the house and also the garden. Before stepping out into the street he stretched out his arm and picked a handful of jasmine flowers from a bush's branch that had climbed up the gate's posts. Tonio joined their stems together, inhaled their fragrance, and pinned them into his light brown flannel coat's boutonniere.

The Striscia's streets were almost deserted. He only met two or three sea-captains. On the Striscia everyone was a captain. Occasionally someone admitted to being a boatswain but never a simple sailor. Whoever came to live on the Striscia, even if he was a dry-cleaner, was given the honorary title of sea-captain to an invisible fleet. Tonio strolled down Rome Street and passed by the Academic Club. He wasn't in the mood to go in there and either debate about Nietzsche or kill time playing cards.

He went to People's Square and walked down Seas Street that lead directly to the shoreline's cliffs. The street was deserted. In the pale light coming from the half moon and the feeble street lamps, he fell inward and began to ruminate. His mother's superstitions kept coming into his mind and he fought them off with his enlightened barrage of arguments. She wasn't the only superstitious one. He knew there were many in town who believed in even more outrageous superstitions than his mother's. In the past he too had been a fool and had believed in piles of rubbish. Now he knew better. His mind's eyes had penetrated through the thick clouds of falsehoods, illusions, superstitions, myths, dogmas, axioms, both honest and dishonest assumptions, and found a clear view of things as they really are. He had come to the conclusion that the universe had no apparent reason and that humanity had a past but no future. He remembered the time he too was groping in the darkness. Before that he had been caught in the false goals of a life full of adventure. The void of ignorance had to be filled somehow.

First he had wanted to become a pilot, but his mother forbade him to do so. The airplanes of that time were too flimsy a means to ply the skies. The seas were still treacherous, but could be mastered, he thought. By age twelve he had learned some geography, astronomy, and how to use a sextant. His mariner's dream quickly fell apart the first day he went out on his father's fishing trawler. He literally found out he didn't have the stomach for it. Tonio had no other choice but to build his future on firm land. Unfortunately the land he and his mother had in mind was the land of literary fiction, an imaginary Arcadia with a soft and freely yielding soil, a sky without a cloud in it, and a life as pleasant as a perennial fete-champetre. In that imaginary paradise theme park there were neither offices nor factories stinking with the sweat of those who were breaking their backs within their walls for their daily bread. Naturally there couldn't be farms and farmers laboring from dawn until sunset and beyond. With Arcadia in mind, mother and son forced Giovanni, the father, to commute twenty kilometers to the Striscia to go out to sea from the village of Uttoli where they had bought a cottage with a tiny garden. Tonio was fifteen then and still reading the works of Bernardin de Saint Pierre- in French, of course. Evidently his desires had been influenced by Romantic literature.

His fifteen year old's concept of love required a certain type of rural girl, a setting of glens and brooks, and of course plenty of moonlight. In such a bucolic setting Tonio searched for a girl with a pure soul who, like him, longed for the rural life. As in any respectable idyl Tonio's expectation of finding a rural love was soon fulfilled. On one of his morning wanderings through the meadows he strayed farther than he had intended to and the hot midday sun caught him in the open fields searching for a shelter. He crossed a path flanked by bougainvillea heading for the shade of a huge carob tree. When he reached the tree he found that someone else was already there, taking refuge from the scorching sun. It was a farm girl who looked about his age, beautiful beyond compare, with hair like the sea of wheat waving gently under the light breeze in the plain stretching endlessly in front of him. Tonio immediately fell in love with the girl, Paluzza Oliveri, such was her name, at first sight. Soon they became inseparable for the rest of the summer. Tonio never bothered to ask Paluzza whether she was a native of Uttoli. It was apparent to him that she was a local country girl, and it would have been such a stupid question to ask her. Tonio would have liked to accompany Paluzza home after having spent much of the day with her, to meet the farmer and his wife, the proud parents of such a beautiful girl. Paluzza never let him near her cottage, "out of modesty," he thought.

Every evening by the stone fence that enclosed her front yard they stopped holding hands and separated from each other . Tonio watched Paluzza from her first step on the short path that led to the green door. They would meet again in the afternoon under the carob tree. She would appear to him to be lovelier than the day before. Tonio attributed the miracle of Paluzza's physical beauty to the healthy environment nature had provided, unspoiled by the polluting fumes and waste from factories and mills. He also attributed the beauty of her soul to the simplicity of the country's goals, so different from the materialistic aspirations fostered by the city. Tonio not only loved Paluzza, he also loved her surroundings, her plain attire, her artless ways, her attachment to the land. In his eyes she was nature's purest daughter. When Paluzza consented, he held her tight in his arms and got inebriated by her wild flower scent. They infallibly met every afternoon under the carob tree and made love. Unfortunately for the lovers, time was flying away. Fall was fast approaching and soon they would have to part, to meet again next year. Perhaps.

The painful day of departure soon arrived. Tonio and Paluzza said good-bye to each other under the carob tree, of course, on an ideal evening that seemed made for romantic souls. The moon was shining in the starry sky, the brook was murmuring lovers' melodies, the bell of the chapel on the hill was chiming the end of the day. But they had to return home. They sobbed madly for the last time, and with tears in their eyes swore to love each other forever. They parted with the solemn promise to meet again next year and a year's time seemed to them longer than an eternity.

It came as an incredible surprise to both of them to meet again on the Striscia only a couple of days after their separation at Uttoli. It was the greatest disappointment of Tonio's life. Paluzza was in fact a city girl. He had fallen in love with a summer vacationer, a girl from the Striscia, and an offspring, like him, of a sea-captain. For him the enchantment of the Arcadian love was broken forever. The country girl he had fallen in love with had never existed. The girl now in front of him didn't stir either a single muscle in his flesh or a single sparkle in his imagination. On the other hand, Paluzza was extremely glad to find out that her lover was, after all, from her own turf and that she didn't have to wait for a year to see him again. They would resume their hot romance right away. Besides, she had come to know he wasn't a farm boy as she had presumed, but a student at the Liceo. She could introduce him to her parents after all. At Uttoli she hadn't dared to, believing her parents wouldn't possibly have approved of her being infatuated with a farm boy.

Chapter III

Paluzza commented to herself, "I should have suspected Tonio, with his smooth manners, and his punctilious syntax couldn't have been a farmer boy, although he did always wear plain broadcloth cotton shirts, denim trousers and heavy leather boots." Those boots were in fact killing his feet, and whenever he could, he took them off with a sigh of relief.

"Those were clear signs to everyone else but me that he wasn't from the country. Anyway that's all in the past. The important thing is that we are here together and madly in love with each other. God knows how much I love this handsome, tall boy. It's true he has a few crazy ideas in his head, but nobody's perfect after all." But soon after they had returned to the Striscia, Paluzza noticed that a change had occurred in Tonio's behavior toward her. He hadn't hugged and kissed her as passionately as be had done at Uttoli, under the carob tree. "It's because we're here under the scrutiny of too many eyes, and Tonio's so shy," Paluzza reasoned. Fortunately for her they spent a lot of time together as the Liceo and the Ginnasio they attended were in the same quadrangle which had formerly comprised the old abbey. In the morning they went to school together and later they often returned home together, but the balance sheet of their romance showed a deficit of expressed affection. Paluzza counted the days to the next summer when they could return to Uttoli. She didn't take the hint that Tonio's coldness was his silent way of telling her that all was over between them. More than once Tonio was on the point of telling Paluzza he didn't love her anymore and as a matter of fact lately she had been a pain in the ass, but he couldn't bring himself to be so brutally blunt. He searched for an occasion and a way to gently break the news to her. As time went on things unfortunately grew worse. Whenever Paluzza grew tenderly passionate and asked him how much he loved her, he would lie to her and tell her that he loved her more than ever. Afterwards he hated himself for his duplicity. Besides, he had to stand his mother's nagging for not being capable of breaking off his relationship with a mere fisherman's daughter. His mother couldn't stand fishermen, her own husband included.

"What am I going to do?" Tonio was asking himself as month after month went by and he was still procrastinating telling Paluzza what he should have told her the first time they met at the

Striscia. As summer was now upon them he had a chance to put some distance between himself and Paluzza. Through the mediation of friends he got a counselor's job at the boys summer camp in Alcamo Ilarino, a hundred kilometers from the Striscia. Unfortunately for Tonio when he returned in the Fall, he found out that nothing had changed for Paluzza. She still hadn't forgotten him as he had hoped, nor had she set eyes on anyone else, although there were many boys eager to love her. Tonio's mother, seeing his inability to straighten things out by himself, decided more than once to intervene but Tonio put his foot down to save his self-respect. It was his business and nobody else's. Now, even his old grandmother had stepped into the picture. But the rich old lady had taken Paluzza's part in the dispute instead, and even threatened to change Tonio's status as her sole beneficiary of her Will unless he married a fisherman's daughter like herself.

"What's keeping you from dropping Paluzza?" his mother taunted him. "Is all that grandma's money tempting you?" Tonio denied that that was the reason, but it took him seven years to summon enough courage to tell Paluzza that their love had lasted for only one summer, and now nothing at all remained of that brush-fire. Even it's ashes had been blown away by the wind. It was the most painful thing he had ever done in his life.

Chapter IV

Six months had already passed since that awful day he and Paluzza were free to go their separate ways. "Which is my way?" Tonio asked himself, walking down Seas Street on that evening hour almost deserted except for a dog, a polychrome mongrel with long ears and a short tail, that was preceding him on the sidewalk. The dog roamed and sniffed everything and everywhere, and at each stop pissed again and again. "The poor dog's diabetic." Tonio sighed. His sympathy for the ailing dog didn't last long. He cursed the beast as soon as he stepped right into the poor animal's excrement. Tonio cleaned his shoes with a piece of paper and resumed his walk. To him the topography of the universe was an outrageous maze, topped by routes so crazily laid and leading nowhere.

"That lie," he thought, "any drunken human being couldn't have done any worse." It showed indifference, stupidity, and wickedness to such a high degree that it excluded any rational concern or purpose.

"How am I going to live a purposeless life?" he asked himself again and again. How do I anesthetize my mind from the painful thoughts of decay and death? Coliseums, skyscrapers, science, arts, religions, states, wheels, turbines, lenses, telecommunications, Pyramids, temples, cathedrals, all inventions past and future had, have, and will have the cogent purpose of anesthetizing minds from the painful thoughts of death. The efforts we make to alleviate our pains and tribulations on the brief journey from the cradle to the tomb are all vanity," Tonio concluded, "my train of thought included."

"Why did I refuse to marry Paluzza? Is it really because I didn't feel any passion for her? That was my excuse. It seems so banal. Is passion the product of literary fiction fostered by bourgeois categories? And yet I have made love to women who also didn't inspire passion and I didn't seem to have missed it. Why did I insist that Paluzza have this idle literary quid? Because I am crazy."

Thus, Tonio reached the Lungomare and went to sit on a wrought-iron bench a few feet away from the sea. Six months earlier he recalled, sitting on the same bench, he had told Paluzza, in rather oblique language, that he didn't love her anymore. He had also told her he was going to Spain to fight in the civil war there. Paluzza hadn't followed his obscure circumlocutions closely and hadn't understood a single word he was saying. When she finally realized he was telling her that all was over between them and that this was a good-bye, she fainted in his arms. When she regained consciousness she cried and sobbed for the entire evening. His words had gone beyond breaking their relationship, they had cut deeply into her being. Her words echoed, "My God, do I disgust you to the point you prefer Spain and death to a life here with me? Am I worse than death in your eyes?" she asked him. It can't be so, she consoled herself. There must be another woman in his life. Anyway after seven years of waiting for him she couldn't let another woman take him away from her. She wondered who it could be? Paluzza, couldn't come up with the vaguest idea who her mysterious rival was. She imagined the other woman as very beautiful, very rich, and well educated, while she herself had grown fat, without a penny to her own name and had dropped out of school. Thus she was at great disadvantage in comparison. At least she could have gotten a good education hadn't it been for her dumb father, who thought with his wet bottom rather than with his head. He had forced her to drop out of school by telling her that an educated woman makes a bad wife.

"What does a stupid fisherman know about what makes a good wife?" Paluzza cried out.

Your mother's behind this, isn't she? She never liked me," she raged to Tonio.

"What are you talking about?" he snapped back.

"That your mother succeeded in breaking up our relationship, finally. She's trying to stop it by sending you to Spain," she screamed at him.

"Paluzza, please don't shout. My mother might have interfered in our relationship but she doesn't know anything about my intention of going to Spain. If you don't stop shouting somebody's bound to hear you, and I could be sent to the wall and shot as a traitor,"

Tonio besought her.

"Go to Spain, then! Mamma's boy, but if you ever return home alive you'll still be mine. I'd rather kill you than see you with another woman. Remember my words!" Paluzza left after uttering her menacing promise.

Tonio knew that she meant every word of it. Six months had gone by since then and Tonio had changed his mind about going to fight in Spain.

Learning of his change of heart from mutual friends, "He's a fickle bastard," Paluzza commented. "Nothing lasts more than a season with him."

Tonio knew that Paluzza was shadowing him or had her spies wherever he went. As he hadn't taken up with any other woman he felt safe from Paluzza's promise to kill him if she ever caught him with another woman. Even now, while sitting on the bench, he guessed she was nearby. He turned his head and saw her familiar silhouette appear and disappear from behind the spruces.

"Poor girl, try to forget me!" he sighed.

Elvira Damiani Giaccone didn't know that Paluzza hadn't given up her claim on her son. She, believing that Tonio was free at last, was earnestly searching for an ideal wife for him. She had searched for months now, and so far hadn't had much luck . Tonio still lived with his parents, in a situation not unusual on the island. In the evening, after supper, his mother had asked Tonio to seek divine guidance on the matter. He should go and consult the Sibyl oracle to know who, and where to find her.

"Holy smoke! How can I ever do that? If Academe ever found out about I'd be thrown to the wolves, and barred from teaching forever," But Tonio owed his mother more than that.

At most it would cost him a dash of embarrassment with his colleagues. A small price for him to pay to make his mother happy. Lately her health had begun to deteriorate fast and he dreaded the prospect of losing her. She was the only person on earth who kept him going. Tonio got up from the bench and headed toward home. If his mother insisted on it he would oblige her and go to the grotto to the oracle of the Sibyl. He would make a fool of himself for his mother's sake.

Chapter V

Turri told the cab-driver to drop him off at the Striscia. He didn't want to go straightaway home for many reasons. First of all, he needed time to let it sink into his head that he hadn't had a dream but he had actually held Princess Carlotta Salinas in his arms. That wasn't all. He had a date with her tonight at ten o'clock. The second reason was he did not know how to break the news to his mother. She would object of course. Thirdly, if he lingered a while also at the rocky beach, it would be too late for his mother to force him to go to his summer job at the pharmacy as he didn't feel in the mood to work today of all days. He didn't have to go to Villa Augusta before ten o'clock and he had plenty of time on his hands.

The Striscia, Turri hadn't been back down there in years. As a little boy he used to go there and watch the fishing-boats going out to sea, their white sails slowly disappearing at the last horizon, or from out there where the sea meets the sky, emerge, each no larger than half a postage stamp cut diagonally and slowly grow larger until they came into port and delivered their catch.

There were now very few sails to be seen on the blue surface. With the sailing culture gone, so also was the Striscia as he had remembered it, with its nomadic-like poetry. On the waterfront there were no more large clay and copper pots cooking bouillabaisse in the open air over two bricks and burning flotsam wood and dry algae. Gone were also the many improvised tents made with oars and spars tied together with galomas and covered with old sails instead of canvasses. In their shade even a stranger was welcome to find relief from the hot sun, and also partake freely of the bouillabaisse, and have a drink of water and often of wine. Neither were there any longer. Neither were the nets, spun by the fishermen's wives and daughters coiled in stacks or being mended by the fishing crew sitting on coiled ropes, all while the old men told old tales of disaster or human endurance at sea.

Turri mostly saw before him large trawlers with all sorts of mechanical aids coming in or going out to sea. They stank of naphta and left the surface of the water murky and oily. They caught more fish with their huge nets in a day than the old sailboats used to catch in a month, and yet fish was more expensive now than ever. Turri walked to the next pier to a spot where some kids and an old man had cast their fishing lines in the murky water, sitting on the granite edge with their feet dangling a few inches above the water. He would have liked to have seen a freshly caught fish.

"Pop, are the salted anchovies biting the bait today or are you after the smoked herrings?" Turri teased the old man.

"No, son. I'm catching canned jerks today," the old man answered without taking his eyes off the line's cork.

"Touche!" Pops, you're razor sharp. When I reach your age I hope I'm as sharp as you are," Turri complimented the old man who kept his eyes on the line. He sat by the fishing group and waited. After a while seeing that nobody was catching anything Turri headed for the rocky beach to settle an old account. No sooner had he reached Manzoni Square than he heard the familiar voice of Professor Tonio Giaccone, his Latin and Greek teacher, calling him. The professor had just come out of Pellegrino's book store and immediately spotted his pupil.

"Jesus! He's got eyes like a hawk," cried Turri to himself, who would have liked to have avoided this encounter with his teacher. "For certain he'll make the same tired old joking accusation of my neglecting my studies," Turri surmised. He crossed the square and went to meet the professor nevertheless.

"Turri, what on earth are you doing here? So that's how you waste your time when you should be home studying for final exams. It won't be long now. Do you expect your professors to give you a passing grade if you don't study and don't have the right answers, counting on friendship instead? Not in your life!" the professor told him bluntly.

"I don't think there is any problem. If I don't have the answers I couldn't care less," Turri answered shrugging his shoulders.

"I can see from your stupid smile that you really don't care whether you pass or not. What's happened to you, have you become an idiot?"

"Professor, I don't have to listen to anymore of it."

"I liked you better when you were pitifully morose than so stupidly happy as you are now. What's happened to you?"

"Something good. You don't like seeing me happy, do you? It bothers you to see happy people around you. Look what you've done to poor Paluzza!"

"Turri, mind your own business!"

"And you, likewise. Good-bye, Professor Giaccone!"

Tonio was astonished by Turri's vehement language and unusual behavior. He watched Turri disappear into the crowd.

"Youth's unpredictable moods," he sighed. "I

bet he's so happy because he's on his way to see Marianne Buzzuni. I guess she finally gave into him," he ruminated while heading for the Academic Club.

"Neither you, Professor Tonio Giaccone, nor anybody else can dampen my happiness today," Turri commented to himself while heading for the rocky beach. He fished into his trousers pocket and found the keys to the back gate of Villa Augusta. "This is the key to my actual and future happiness," he felt like shouting at every passerby he met. "I want to get to the rocky beach in a kind of pilgrimage of defiance of all of the unhappy memories it holds for me, now that I am a winner. I want to shout out my happiness to those goddamn rocks and that water that I now detest. I want to shout out to that bitch Antoinette del Lago whom I met there and who preferred an old bastard to me; and out to the repulsive Giulia Manna and her revolting layers of lard; to Marianne Buzzuni, oversized of body and short of brains; to the late old fool Carlo Mazzetti who ridiculed my dreams of conquest. I am a conqueror, you old fool, not of Empires but of beautiful princesses. Only six months ago I crossed these streets with a crushed spirit. Now all is reversed. I see things in a different perspective now that the thick clouds of darkness which overshadowed my life have been finally dispelled by that bright star, Carlotta Salinas. I can hope for a bright future and true happiness. I can see that there is a bit of good in the world and I'm going to get the best part of it," he resolved.

Chapter VI

"I WILL MARCH STRAIGHT NO MATTER WHAT LIES AHEAD"

Turri read the sign inscribed on one of the walls of the brown brick De Simone Tile Company building, and his blood pressure didn't shoot way up as it always had in the past. He remembered that old fool Carlo Mazzetti's remark. "Go ahead, you dummy, follow what the sign says. The lake's right in front of your path."

"It's the sea, rather, you old fool. There, it is the Mare Nostrum, Our Sea," he had replied.

"Not so fast, buddy! It's not our sea. There are others who lay claim on it also. It's not ours at, all."

"It was ours once."

"But if you go back a few million years there was no sea at all. When it became a sea long before man came along, it belonged to all creatures great, and small."

"It's our sea, I'm telling you. Anyway why do

you have to make a federal case out of anything I say?"

"You are an ass," were the old man last words.

Before reaching the intersection between Seas Street and the Lungomare Isonzo, Turri read the other sign on the wall of the Lombardi Ceramics Company. It emphasized the theme of the previous one.

"To live a day as a lion is better than to live a hundred years as a sheep"

The last time he had come this way and read that sign he had been in a bad mood and in a different disposition, he remembered. "I thought of myself as a lion, then. What a jerk I was only a few months ago," he commented to himself while walking on the Lungomare, now almost deserted as always during working hours when the sheep were busy being fleeced within the confines of factories and offices. He had vowed to die of starvation rather to become imprisoned every day of his life within the stark walls of factories and offices. "I believed I was a conqueror." He mused. "Like most of my peers I thought the times were ripe for bold men like me. Our goal was the restoration of the Roman Empire. That old bastard Mazzetti derided my dreams of glory with questions like: 'Do you really believe that the ruins of the Forum, together with the remaining and precariously standing Arches, the few disconnected segments of useless aqueducts standing in the middle of nowhere, the decayed stones of the ancient amphitheaters, so sharp that they can cut your ass if you sit on them without a pillow, all loquerunt in Lingua Latina to Mussolini, and in no uncertain terms cry for the restoration of the Roman Empire?' You damned fools, you'd better leave the past alone!"

"That old cretin can't understand history's cogent imperatives," I used to comment disgusted. The restoration of the Empire was an immense task that required strong men like myself," I thought. "At times I felt inadequate to the task because I was so in love and I thought that soldiers can't afford to be in love.

"I really was in love with Princess Carlotta Salinas. Ever since I saw Carlotta, who really embodies the perfect form of womanhood, no other girl has been at all able to dislodge her lovely vision from my mind. No other girl compares even distantly with Carlotta. I fell in love with her the first time I saw her, but my low status and the countless obstacles I knew how hopeless my dream of love was. Regardless of the few distractions from my fixation with Carlotta I'd found with other girls, my heart has always remained anchored at Princess Salinas' feet. That is, figuratively, until this morning. Many times I'd dreamt that I really was at Villa Augusta and that I really was at Carlotta's feet. If you haven't been branded by love, and your flesh and your soul haven't been singed by its red-hot iron, you won't understand this overwhelming urge to be your lover's slave. In your miserable state you wish for any merciful act of compassion on her part toward you. Sometimes in my dreams this wish is granted. Carlotta sees me at her feet compassionately and gives me a hand and lifts me slowly up. On my rising from the floor I embrace and kiss first her ankles, then her knees, her thighs, her bosom, until I get to stand up and holding her in my arms finally I kiss her silky lips. That dream will come true tonight at last. I've to confess that while sleepwalking through the last two years with Carlotta's vision in my mind, I've played pranks on a few girls, but I've never tried to seduce any of them with one exception: the big, buxom blonde Marianne Buzzuni. I am not in love with her. I simply had tried to give my mind a few minutes of rest from the recurrent thoughts of Carlotta. However, Marianne has been reluctant to oblige me. Anna Tascone is the other girl besides Carlotta who stirs my imagination at all. There is a striking resemblance between Carlotta and Anna. Besides their ages the other difference between them is the color of the hair, Ann being a blonde. Anyway, it was on an afternoon like this that I was heading this way for the rocky beach to get the rage I was in out of my system because of Giulia's accusation. I was directed to my usual rocky solitary spot. Unfortunately at times I had to share it with Carlo Mazzetti, a pest of an old man. I hoped that Mazzetti wouldn't be there as I needed peace rather than disputation with an old cretin so deadly opposed to the restoration of the Roman Empire.

"What has he got to lose from it? Is he not one of us? Hasn't he, like everyone of us born on this land, laden with history and artifacts of ancient civilizations, found direction for the future in the trail of the past? Evidently he has lost his marbles and is drifting aimlessly without any historical references. He's unaffected by the remaining old temples at Acragas, Seline, Segesta. Aren't these old stones his? On the banks of the Nile, the Euphrates, the Ganges, the Yangtze, there are stones older than these, but these are our stones, our inspiration the roots of our future. We should get rid of the old traitor Mazzetti," Turri concluded.

In the bad mood he was in he would have easily disposed of the old man if he happened to be at the secluded rocky beach. It took him an hour to walk the tree kilometers from the harbor to the beach. From the distance of half a kilometer he spotted Mazzetti standing on the uneven rocks.

"I'll kill him!" he cried, frustrated. "How do I get rid of him?" he asked myself. He looked around and saw nobody in sight. "This is a propitious moment to push that old bastard down the cliff and let him drown after he hits the rocks below. I am sure he won't survive either the impact of the fall on the sharp edges of the rocks or the frothing vortex of the surf." He pondered on the chances he had of getting away with it. "Nobody will ever know the truth," he thought.

"It will be thought an accident caused by a spell of dizziness or by a gust of wind," he concluded. I looked around again, and seeing no one in sight, he decided to do it for his country. Avoiding the least noise he got closer and closer to Mazzetti who either remained absorbed contemplating the sea or was lost completely in reverie with his back turned to his assailant. Turri's throat had become so dry by the great emotion he was in that if he had screamed no sound would have emerged out of his mouth. His breathing had become heavily irregular and louder as he got closer to the old man. He couldn't check it. "I'm breathing louder than a car with a busted muffler," He joked in an effort to ease it. Not a chance. If the surf's noise hadn't covered my noisy breathing it would have given me away. He counted the distance that separated him from Mazzetti. "Another five steps, four, three, two, one, push!"

He told myself. He closed his eyes and extended his arms to push Mazzetti to his death. With his knuckles he almost touched the old man's maroon corduroy coat. Instantly he withdrew his hands. He couldn't do it. "Am I a coward?" He asked himself, horrified at the thought of admitting it. "Until then I had thought I could kill a person if I had to. When the moment to test my guts came my courage failed me. My God, I am a coward!" Full of shame he wanted to die by jumping down off the cliffs. Then he tried to redeem his cowardice by mastering a second attempt, but Mazzetti foiled it by turning around: and facing him. He had sensed that someone had unexpectedly come behind his back to harm him.

"That's that stupid kid again," Mazzetti sighed with regret. "I've tried to steer him away from evil and he pays me back by trying to kill me. Now the criminal is running away," he sighed seeing Turri leaving the scene of the abortive crime as, fast as he could. Turri was puzzled and demoralized. "If I am not a man of action, what am I good for? Nothing," he concluded, broken hearted. "At best I'll end up behind a desk since I don't have any artistic inclinations. The time's come to say good-bye to dreams of glory. I've been a sheep disguised as a lion all this time. Now I can't pretend anymore. Now I have to think of how to eke out a living like a good sheep should.

Besides being covered by my friends' ridicule. I'll have to crack the books or I'll end up digging ditches. While my peers build the new Empire I'll be buried alive in an office somewhere. It will be hard on me seeing them building the Empire without me. I'll share the shame with any coward who won't dare participate in the glorious event, and like him:

> Grieve forever
> When retelling
> His children
> The event
> Sighing has to admit:
> I wasn't there
> On the day of glory.
> I didn't rally
> Under our flag.

From now on I'll be spending my free time at the Public Library, delving into the civil lore and closing the pages of Thucydides, Xenophon, Caesar, Woban, and Napoleon forever. I'll have to exchange the sword for the ballpoint pen. But I don't have the guts to tell Peter, Geo, Paul, and my courageous friends that I'm a coward. I'll pretend for a while to be what I am not. Gradually I'll drop out of their company and join Tommaso, Angelo, Gaetano, and the others who can only dream of noble deeds. What can I do? I feel like an eagle whose wings have been clipped and can't soar into the sky's infinite space anymore. I am obliged to crawl up on the earth and preach the virtue of that crawling. In fact I feel like a destitute small version of Lucifer who in the wink of an eye fell from the purity of Heaven into the mud of Earth." Turri blushed at the crudity of his past ideals.

Chapter VII

Walking under the Buzzuni's balcony Turri smiled thinking of the prank he played on Marianne a year or so ago. Turri wasn't in love with Marianne Buzzuni although the big body of the blonde was catching his eye. She enjoyed provoking him whenever she was at the balcony and he happened to walk under it. She always came so close to the wrought-iron balustrade that her skirt got caught between the iron ornaments and was lifted so high that he could see her thighs and the color of her underwear. A little at a time she built in Turri the urge to possess her huge body and he began lying to Marianne that he had fallen in love with her and couldn't go on living without her love. Marianne was somewhat soft in the head but very hard in her determination to resist Turri's advances. One evening Turri tried to seduce Marianne in her own house, while her parents were out. The attorney Buzzuni and his wife returned home in time to prevent their daughter from being "raped by the over-roused punk" as he put it. The huge bald attorney chased Turri out of his house and vowed to kill him if he ever set foot in it again. Turri didn't give up, though. "I was forbidden to set foot in your home again,! he kept telling Marianne on the telephone, "but if you love me, you must come and see me either on the medieval ramparts or at the rocky part of the beach. Will you come this evening?"

"I'll try. Wait, for me at the ramparts after sunset."

"That's what you told me last Friday and the Friday before that and then you didn't show up. Are you sure you will come this time? Come, please!"

"I'll try," answered Marianne.

"Good, I'll wait for you there," a jubilant Turri told her. At dusk he went to the ramparts and waited for Marianne. He waited for hours and as usual Marianne didn't come to meet him there. Turri was very disappointed and thought out a plan of revenge. He had found an old revolver in the attic and had managed to get some blank cartridges. He confided his plan to his friend Tom Pistuni. The joke was set for next Wednesday evening as that was the day that his mother usually went to visit aunt Maria. On Wednesday, as soon as his mother left the house Turri called Marianne on the telephone. As usual he complained to her for not having come to the ramparts, and for her lack of response to his love. "Away from you I'm dying a little each day. To shorten my slow agony I've come to the conclusion that it's best for me to commit suicide. Tonight I'll shoot myself with this revolver that I am holding in my hand."

"Turri, don't! Please! Do you really love me this much that you would die for me?"

"Of course I do. If you tell me you won't elope with me tonight, I'll take it that you don't love me, and I'll discharge all the bullets in this revolver into my temple and my heart."

"Turri, for God's sake, don't do it!"

"Does it mean that you love me and will come with me tonight?"

"I really don't know what to do with you. You ask me to make such a drastic decision with such far-reaching consequences in such a short time. Give me time to think it over first."

"I have given you enough time to think it over. Please, make your decision now! Come away with me tonight, my love. I swear to you you'll never regret leaving your home and your parents for my sake. We'll be happy together wherever destiny tosses us. With you at my side I'll be a great success. Marianne, love, please tell me you love me enough to come away with me tonight. My life depends entirely on your decision. You tell me yes and I'll live. You tell me you refuse means I don't. If you don't love me I'll kill myself. You have three minutes to come to a decision, starting now. If you let the three minutes go by without telling me you'll come, I'll pull the trigger and good-bye forever."

"You're mad, mad, mad!"

"Mad or sane I love you. Thirty seconds have gone by. If you let the other 150 seconds go by in the same way I'll pull the trigger. Marianne, I'm begging you! Come away with me!"

"How can I come with you if I don't know if I am in love with you? I don't even know what love is."

"There isn't time to find out what it is."

"But, if I don't know what love is, how shall know whether I love you or not?"

"Look, if the thought of my death brings you sorrow it means that you love me. Does it?"

"A little."

"Christ, I'm going to die for you and you feel only just a little sorrow for my death? You're so beautiful but also so cruel. Remember that you're sending me to my grave. Good-bye forever!"

Turri pulled the trigger three times, holding the gun so close to the telephone that the three blank shots must have thundered into Marianne's ear like three cannon shots. Turri heard her crying in astonishment.

"Dad! Mom! A horrible accident has happened! Turri shot himself because of me. I'll never forgive myself! He's dead. Oh My God! Turri's dead!" she was screaming. "I heard the shots with my own ears on the telephone. It's all my fault!"

Turri was still holding the receiver in his hand. He heard Marianne crying and sobbing,

"I didn't believe he loved me that much, but he really did. God, forgive me, for having had doubts about it."

When Turri heard Mr. Buzzuni's heavy footsteps getting louder therefore nearer, he hung up. A few seconds later his telephone rang. Turri didn't pick up the telephone, sure that it was Buzzuni calling to inquire about the accident. The telephone rang and rang but Turri didn't answer it. Finally it stopped.

"Mr. Buzzuni got tired of calling or his finger is so sore from dialing he's given up," Turri commented laughing.

The following morning Turri told his mother that he didn't feel well and he didn't go to school. Marianne, not seeing him there, anxiously asked Tom Pistuni about Turri, "what happened to him last night?"

Tom knew all about the jest and scolded her out, "You know better than anybody else that Turri shot himself last night because you jilted him. You played your seduction game perfectly. As soon as he fell into your trap you jilted him. Turri reacted wrongly though. He should have turned the gun on you rather than on himself."

"It's my fault I know, and I'm very sorry that it turned out that way. Tell me, please, is he still alive or is he dead?"

"He's alive. Fortunately the bullets missed his vital parts. The bullets missed his heart but you broke it forever with your insensitivity. From now on find yourself another toy to play with. Human hearts are easily broken but unlike toys can't be as easily repaired."

Marianne ran away in tears. Obviously she confided to a close friend that Turri attempted suicide because she jilted him. The news quickly spread everywhere. The next day Turri appeared in school with bandages around his neck, and with tufts of gauze poking out of his shirt, confirming the rumor of his attempted suicide on Marianne's account. He immediately became a celebrity as the sad symbol of unrequited love. Many girls who before the prank hadn't even noticed that Turri existed now made him the focus of their attention and would willingly console him from his presumed tristesse. At times he was inclined to believe in the image he had helped to create for himself. He stared at himself in the mirror and only saw that he was a fraud. He searched deeper to discover who he really was, what he was." I can't see a damn thing," he commented discouraged. "I only know that I am sick."

Help came to him from an unsuspected

source, Antoinette del Lago. Turri had admired her from afar, thinking that she hadn't found him worthy of any notice. Certainly it had been so in the past. Then on a Friday Antoinette suddenly attached herself to his arm, and in a most friendly way invited him to attend her celebrated Saturday night shindig. Next evening Turri climbed the steps of the del Lago's residence to be made a liege at Antoinette's service. Turri spent an unforgettable night with Antoinette. Holding her in his arms was a quasi-divine experience. Her red hair was inflaming his heart. Her blue eyes promising him the sky. The fragrance and texture of her flesh spelled happiness if only, she would bestow it on him. She didn't. Neither that night nor on the successive nights. He attended many of her Saturday night shindigs and finally realized that she didn't love him enough to give herself to him either. He also found out that Antoinette made the same vague promise of love to every young man there but couldn't bring herself to deliver on the promise. "Is there something wrong with us or with her?" he ruminated. Searching deeply into his heart Turri came to the conclusion that he could live without Antoinette's love. Besides he had had more than enough of the splendor of the miniature Versailles and torn between two impossible dreams of love he opted to be a beggar at the gate of Villa Augusta and at the lovely feet of Princess Carlotta Salinas rather than at those ugly huge ones of Antoinette del Lago. He began visiting the beach again. Now he was the only one to go there since old man Mazzetti had died. Turri stopped reminiscing and walking now under Maxianne's balcony and he was again tempted to lift his head and stare at Marianne's impeccable thighs. He decided against it. Carlotta's thighs were finer still and tonight he would have a chance, to caress their silky smoothness. Thus Turri pretended that he didn't notice Marianne was out, and walked down the street without turning his head or greeting her.

"You gigantic bitch, go to Hell!" he muttered. "Give those large charms of yours which you fortunately for your sake denied me, to a carnivorous beast who prefers quantity to quality. Did you ever realize that your rejection wasn't the catastrophe of my life as I had deliberately made it appear? "Your chicken-brain will eventually comprehend what it was, only a joke for me. I was stabbed through the heart but not under your balcony— and not by you." Thus ruminating, Turri reached the spot of beach he had held so dearly in the past. To his surprise a girl was swimming there . His first impulse was to scare the hell out of her so she wouldn't come back there ever again. Turri changed his mind the moment she came out of the water. He was struck by her beauty veiled by a skimpy yellow bikini. She couldn't compare in beauty to Princess Salinas. The princess was a rare and expensive greenhouse orchid. This girl was a most beautiful wild flower of the field. Turri noticed a striking resemblance between her and Antoinette del Lago, except that her hair was brown, and her skin was delicate and free from freckles. She climbed the cliffs and went to sit on a smooth rock not far from him. She greeted him with a smile. Turri took courage and went to sit by her. Turri told her of her resemblance to Antoinette del Lago . She answered that it shouldn't surprise him as they were cousins and both bore the same name Antoinette del Lago. They began a small talk. Slowly they turned it into a serious conversation and found out many things about each other. Evidently he was an idealist and she, to his regret, was a realist. "We will compromise," he told himself, "and will live happily ever after."

Turri wanted to know how come he hadn't seen her at her cousin's Saturday night shindigs. Before he had a chance to ask her about it she had put her clothes back on, walked to her old Fiat, and was soon gone. It seemed to Turri the 'beach without'. Antoinette was left a dark void. An eclipse had occurred.

The next morning they met again at the beach. Turri in dismay noticed a great change in Antoinette's disposition toward him. Her friendliness and the warm of the day before were gone. She was now coldly polite. Turri didn't know how to handle the situation. He played his part by ear. "Out of the blue she created this glacial atmosphere and I will follow suit by turning myself into ice, too," he decided angrily. Antoinette dived in the water oblivious that he was there. Turri didn't join her. He remained up above trying to pay her back in kind by ignoring her and her doings. He didn't succeed. His plan collapsed within thirty seconds. That was how long his determination lasted to turn his back on her forever. He turned around and stared at her. While he was thus humiliating himself before her, the cruel thief of his heart was swimming, diving, splashing, totally ignoring he was there or existed. "Is there any justice?" he questioned the heavens. "She's free to ignore me. Why shouldn't I be able to do likewise? No, I can't. I can't concentrate on anything but her. I'm vanquished, a slave at her feet, but she won't lighten my chains or raise me from the dust."

Turri saw Antoinette coming out of the water, climbing the cliffs, sitting on that smooth rockland drying herself with a white towel. She put her clothes back on uttered coldly a good-bye, and left. Her behavior turned Turri into a stone. However he didn't give up hope that she would shed her inexplicable gloom and return his love.

The next day Turri went to the beach and waited for Antoinette. Two hours went by and she failed to appear. Another half hour passed and Turri despaired of her coming there that day. Finally he heard the asthmatic breathing of her Fiat getting loud and louder, then silence. "She's arrived, thank God," he sighed relieved, but he didn't go to meet her. He remained crouched down on her favorite rock, facing the sea. He heard her footsteps approaching but he didn't turn his head toward the newcomer. "What an impolite welcome I am giving my love," he rebuked himself. "I'm a fool. I'm dying to see her, to oblige her to, love her, to ask her to be mine forever, and what do I do instead? I give her the false impression that I don't care whether she's coming or going. Because of my stupid pride I'm going to lose her."

Antoinette stopped near Turri and still standing asked him,

"How are you to-day?"

"Fine," he answered her coldly without turning toward her. From his position he could not see much of Antoinette, only an edge of her light-brown silk dress, her slender calves, and her high-heel chamois shoes.

Evidently she won't be enter the water today with these trappings on," he thought while Antoinette managed without his help to sit next to him without soiling her attire. "At her young age she dresses like some old broad," Turri commented to himself. He was dying to look at her. To accomplish this he faked an itch on his left shoulder and turned his body a little toward Antoinette. "God, she's more beautiful than I had noticed!" he said taking a quick look at her, and returning to his previous position with his hands stretched apart for keeping his equilibrium. Both remained silent.

"Should I open up my heart to her?" he pondered. "No, she probably will laugh at me."

They kept staring at the sea. After a long while he felt her soft, beautiful hand touch his left hand. Turri then couldn't pretend any longer. He grabbed her hand, turned around, put his arms around her waist and kissed her lips. They remained in each other's arms for a long while. They could remain like that forever. Time, however, doesn't bend to lovers' wishes. Soon it was time for her to go home. He helped her up from the rocks to the Lungomare. He saw her to her car and watched it disappear into the distance. Turri remained at the beach for another while. Soon the stars appeared in the diaphanous sky. He lifted his head toward them. He was happy. Only the sky was immense enough to comprehend the immensity of the joy he felt down in his heart. He returned home as happy as his mother had ever seen him. He wanted to tell her the reason for his happiness, but he didn't. He wanted to tell her later. For the moment he wanted to taste the joy of being in love all by himself, as it was a fragile creation that needed a period of solidification before being exposed to the public.

The next day Turri hurried to the beach earlier than usual. He was impatient to see his lover again. He waited and waited. At sunset he was still waiting for Antoinette. When the incipient night turned into full darkness he returned home. He went to the beach the next day and waited and waited for her. Antoinette didn't show up. Turri was puzzled. He blamed himself for having fouled things up. "It's my fault," he scolded himself. "I should have had her promise to come back . I didn't even tell her that I love her. What a jerk I was..My stupid tongue was tied up. How is she supposed to know what I feel for her if I don't speak up. And yet, were words necessary? Didn't we express silently what we felt for each other much better than words can ever do? Probably she regretted having let me love her. I don't know what to think anymore," he sighed in great pain.

Turri continued going to the beach and waited for Antoinette.

Two weeks went by and Antoinette seemed to have forgotten the beach and her lover. Then Turri's hope was renewed. He noticed her Fiat parked, almost impossible to be seen from the cliffs, behind a field of reeds. Turri, full of joy, ran on the sandy dunes toward the car. Antoinette finally had come back. When, short of breath, he came close to the car he noticed to his dismay that Antoinette was trying to get away before he reached her. "She's avoiding me," he realized with his heart going into pieces. "Why? What have I done wrong?" he asked himself. He had come so close to the car that she couldn't speed away pretending not having seen him. She turned off the ignition and alighted from the car. Turri walked toward her slowly. His heart was broken and his mind confused. He couldn't explain either her long absence or her behavior now that she had come back. He hugged and kissed her passionately in an effort to stir in her the fire of a love that seemed to have turned into ashes. She remained cold and indifferent.

"What's the matter?" he asked her anxiously.

"I shouldn't have come back here," she answered him.

"Why not? Have I caused you a lot of pain?" asked Turri.

"No. You made me very happy."

"So have you."

"We shouldn't have shared that joy. You see I wasn't as free as I pretended to be. I'm engaged to somebody else and soon I'll be married."

Turri couldn't believe what he heard. "It can't

be," he cried in anguish. "If you love me as much as I love you marrying somebody else is out of the question. What's the hurry anyway?" he told her in a barrage and in self defense.

"I don't love him but I have to marry him because he's rich and my family needs his help. He's Giovanni Barracca."

"It can't be. Giovanni Barracca's older than these rocks."

"I know that."

"He's ugly and immoral."

"I know that, too."

"Are you marrying him only because he's rich?"

"Yes."

"You're a bitch!" Turri shouted angrily.

"Can I go now?"

"You can go to Hell for all that I care."

"In that case good-bye!"

"No! Please! Don't go! I didn't mean what I said."

"I've got to go. I'll be back tomorrow and explain. I'll see you tomorrow," she said flatly getting into her car and she vanished behind a cloud of smoke. Turri went home late that night. His mother scolded him for the scandalous hours he came back for supper. To punish him she didn't bother to heat up the cold fish soup. It was as cold as his heart. He went to bed and could not fall asleep. "What good will any explanation of hers be to me? She's decided to marry that old rich bastard. Why should I go to the beach and listen to the excuses why she'll sell herself? The fact remains that she put herself up for sale. This goddamn world's in a worse shape than I thought." It was dawn when he finally fell asleep.

The next day Turri decided not to go to the beach. When the time came he changed his mind and he went. There he hid himself among the reeds. He wanted to see what Antoinette would do when she found out he had stood her up. He concealed himself in the field of reeds in a position from where he could see her if she came and he waited. After a while he heard a car approaching. It wasn't her usual asthmatic Fiat. She came instead in this beautiful Mercedes Benz. "Part of the price of her sale," he commented bitterly. Antoinette alighted from the car and walked toward the cliffs. "My God, how beautiful she looks in that aqua colored silk dress, all perfumed and chic," he thought. Then he saw her venturing onto the rocks in high-heels.

"Jesus, she'll kill herself," he worried. Fortunately she made it. Not seeing Turri there she waited for him. Now and then she checked the time on her wrist-watch. Finally she realized that Turri wouldn't come. "The s.o.b. stood me up," she shouted angrily, "He won't have another chance!"

She managed to get on to the street and back to the car. She left immediately. Turri came out of his hiding place and ran after the speeding car, shouting in despair,

"Don't go! Come back! I'm here! I love you! Do you hear me? I love you!" She either didn't notice him or it didn't bother her that he was chasing after her. In a few seconds the Mercedes was out of sight. Turri was in a state of shock. He had lost the woman he loved forever. For hours he rambled unconsciously. When he finally reopened his eyes to reality he found he was in Acragas among the old Greek Temples. Somehow he had gotten there. He stood in front of the Temple of Concordia. On his left were visible in the darkness broken by a pale moonlight, the Temple of Heracles and that of Olympian Zeus. Farther ahead was the Sea Gate from where he probably had come in. On his right Turri distinguished the Temple of Hera Lacinia. "Why did I come here?" he asked himself. "Perhaps because I'm ruins like these Temples of the forgotten past. Tourists come here, admire the Temples' structures that have survived twenty-seven centuries and they wonder. They remain here an hour or a day and then are gone. Their vision of the past seen from these hills soon intermingles with hundred of other visions from other places and soon is lost in the obscure labyrinth which encloses all forgotten memories. For me and the others born and brought up at the foot of these hills the past's always present and its vision obscures the present. Perhaps it's this perennial vision of the past, together with an education emphatically classical that makes us children of this island anachronistically useless to today's reality and circumstances."

Turri stared once more at the Temple of Concordia. Without a doubt it was beautiful and a historic landmark, but anachronistic. Its architecture had been surpassed by the arch, the dome, the vault.. Its stones had been substituted by steel, concrete, glass, plastic.

"My mind's as full of anachronistic notions as the ideas that you, old temple, embody. The concepts and values which guide my life aren't those of the actual post-industrial world. Love for me has connotations of a past era. For Antoinette's love I'd have sold my soul to the devil. When I was very young I read probably in Maeterlinck, a story of love that I understood. It was about a man and his wife, persecuted for some reason by Caesar. Both of them lived on the run, fleeing from traps and roadblocks most of the time. Finally their luck ran out and they were caught and brought in chains before Caesar. He condemned them to death. Before being taken away the woman told Caesar, "my husband and I have lived all these years worse than savage beasts, without rest, without a roof above our heads, without the necessities of life because of you. And yet we have been happier together in our circumstances than you on this splendor of the throne will ever be." This was the kind of love that I was ready to give and wanted in return from Antoinette. Instead she put riches before love. Old temple, both of us are superfluous in the actual world. Your gods have long vanished from the people's conscience, and your structure can't shelter the tourist from sudden showers.

You're useless both as a shelter for the soul as well as for the body. You're simply remains of the ancient culture that built you and vanished. To what culture do I belong? Perhaps I'm the last member of your vanished congregation, a citizen of this ghost city, with obsolete values impossible to live by in modern conditions. Add to the classic values those of the Judeo-Christian tradition and you have an approximate idea of who I am: a stupid man who believes in a pile of nonsense, romantic love included. I'll let you in on a secret: I still believe that I could walk on water by faith. Unfortunately neither my classicism nor my faith can transmute Lead into Gold. If I had gold, Antoinette, would be mine. Old Temple, tell me, am I barbarian or are the others?" Turri had the commonsense not to wait for an answer.

He rambled for few more hours and somehow made it home. At least he thought so. He sat on the steps of the porch. With his mind in turmoil he had an obfuscated vision of reality, and had somehow mistaken the residence of the other Antoinette del Lago for his own. By chance Antoinette was still up at this late hour of the night. She spotted Turri seated on the steps of her porch in visible disarray. She came down to find out what had happened to him. "Holy smoke! Are you wounded or drunk?" she asked him. "Did you try to make Marianne Buzzuni again and did her father catch you and break every bone in your body?"

"Antoinette, cut it out. Your spirit of potatoes is out of place," he answered her sourly.

"Then it was Marianne herself that chased you!" she teased him while leading him toward the porch's light and had begun to fix his clothes with her beautiful soft hands.

"Sea sand from the shore on your shoes, and sand of the Temples in your hair. Tell me if this isn't evidence that the Amazon chased you all the way from the beach to the temple of Acragas! For five miles! No wonder you're, exhausted. Did she force you to make love to her for hours? She left you moribund."

"Antoinette, please! Cut out this nonsense!"

"Then you're drunk."

"I know it's a disgrace the way I look but I

am not drunk. I just lost my way in the darkness. Lately I've had too many things on my mind. I took a walk and got lost. That's all."

"In the end you've come here."

"I beg your pardon. I shouldn't have come here to bother you this late. Absorbed in thought I wound up here distractedly."

"Turri, don't apologize, please. Evidently your feet led you to the seat of your thoughts. Am I not the cause of your thoughts?" she asked him, assured of her own power over him.

"God, what a conceited broad!" Turri thought. However he didn't want to wound her pride and gave her an ambiguous answer. It is a problem, it's my love for Antoinette del Lago," he told her, meaning her cousin. "Is there any real difference between them? Both are vain and venial," he thought. However his answer pleased Antoinette. She took it to be a veiled proposal of marriage and although pleased by it, she brushed it aside in a polite way. She hugged and kissed him. "Telling me that you love me you made me infinitely happy, but we shouldn't think of marrying soon. We shouldn't rush things. We might have a change of heart. Tonight you're in love with me and I with you, but tomorrow who knows? Therefore let's wait and see if our feelings for each other are of an everlasting kind. Let's not rush into marriage. Let's not mortgage our future so early."

"You are so beautiful and also so wise. I agree with you completely. Let's not spoil our friendship with gushy declarations of eternal love or chains of marriage."

"I knew that you would have understood," she added relieved. Now I won't bother you any longer. I'll go home. Good night, dearest."

"Good night to you, my dear friend," she said hugging and kissing him again.

"God, that was a close call. Thanks, Lord, for having put some sense in his stupid head," she commented.

"Holy smoke, how on earth did she get it into her soft brain that I proposed to her? Thank heavens she rejected me. Now let me see if I can find my way home without any more trouble," ruminated Turri.

Chapter VIII

"It's all in the past now," Turri said to himself staring out at the cliffs. And yet the vision of Antoinette was still there. "You bitch, I'm going to erase you from my memory!" he muttered resentfully at the created image of Antoinette lingering in front of him. He could see her swimming in the water, climbing the cliffs, or sitting on her favorite rock. "Get out of my life, you heartless broad!" he shouted at the phantom. "I don't love you anymore, you little bitch!" he shouted at Antoinette at the top of his lungs, facing the spot in the distance where she now lived. "I don't love you anymore, you whore. Do you hear me? You sold yourself to that old and ugly Barracca. Are you happy? I bet you are, just like a sow in mud. I fell in love with you because I thought you were extraordinary somehow. God, how wrong I was! You proved to be very ordinary—and mercenary to boot. A typist in a law office whose dreams are only of rolling in money at any cost. There must be a billion silly girls like you in this goddamn world who can't go beyond the keyboard of the typewriters in front of them. Their cultural values and sophistication ends right there. Let's blame the environment for all their failings and for yours too. You could have transcended it if you had had any ideals to reach for. I learned the truth that your parents were poverty stricken and that you were born and raised in a hovel. Is that your excuse for having remained a soulless bitch! I wanted you to walk at my side on the road to the stars, but you chose the low road, not knowing or caring about the difference between the two. Money isn't everything. There's love besides, you should know. There's also beauty, style, tinsel, and the illusion of happiness. In a few hours I'll be delving into beauty, happiness, and sophistication all in the arms of a real princess, while you'll be lying beside the decaying and stinking body of an old cadaver. Goodbye, you little bitch," he shouted, then he headed homeward.

Turri got back home just before dinner time. There time stopped. He grew impatient while continuously thinking of Carlotta and of the bliss of love he was going to experience as soon as he got back to Villa Augusta. Fish-soup wasn't his favorite dish and he had always needed his mother's coaxing to finish it, but this afternoon, to his mother's astonishment, he gulped it down in the wink of an eye and went into the living-room. There he sat in front of the pendulum clock counting the seconds and the minutes. Turri had a notion of the theory of relativity of time and now he was experiencing it. From time to time he looked out of the window to see how high the sun was in the sky. It seemed as if it had stopped in the middle of its trajectory and that night would never come. At last the sky turned red and soon it was dark. As soon as the clock struck nine, Turri kissed his mother and hastily was on his way to Villa Augusta. Before leaving it took him a while to make his mother promise him not to worry if he were late coming back home or if he spent the night out. She knew where and with whom Turri would be. Gemma was afraid her son was too young and inexperienced among other things, to find happiness with Princess Carlotta Salinas. She tried to dissuade Turri from keeping the rendezvous, but passion had caught him and she couldn't snap him out of it. Besides her heart told her not to raise the odds higher as they were already too high. Her allegiance was to her son and she ought to be on his side in his fight to conquer the bulwark of prejudice, privilege, and riches, and to snatch away a bit of happiness from their miserly destiny. "Do you need any money?" she asked Turri. He answered with a smile, "I have enough. No thanks, mom. I don't need, cab fare, either. I'll take the bus."

Before Elvira could find fitting words to show

Turri that she now was on his side he was gone. She ran to the window and saw him in the street walking hastily toward the bus-stop. "God," she prayed falling on her knees, "if this is the way that leads my son to his happiness let him get there with thy blessing."

Turri took the bus, only half full at that hour and got off at a stop before Villa Augusta. At the nearest florist he bought a single red rose, then he walked toward the back gate of the villa. He looked around to see if anyone was watching him. The moment he saw that no one was passing by he quickly inserted the key in the lock of the wrought-iron gate. He turned the key until the lock clicked open. Then he cautiously opened the gate, entered the gardens and closed the gate behind him. In the darkness broken only by a pale moonlight, he crossed the walk which was flanked, by tall palm-trees. He made sure not to stray on to the flower-beds to avoid leaving his footprints there. Somehow his steps had assumed a feline-like primordiality of survival against unknown perils. "Primordiality, of my foot," Turri told himself, "the fact is that, I am scared to death by this darkness and by the thought that if Prince Salinas catches me in his daughter's arms he'll kill me." Only a couple of the windows of the immense building were lit but just enough to guide him to the veranda's staircase. He proceeded in the silence that was punctuated by the crickets' chattering and the gushing of unseen fountains.

In no time he reached the foot of the marble staircase, leaned on its railing and looked for Carlotta. She wasn't there waiting for him.

"Did she have a change of heart?" he asked himself disappointed. In that instant he heard her voice whispering from behind a bramble bush, "I'm here." Turri ran toward her. He reached Carlotta, hugged and kissed her. "Are you well, my love?" he inquired anxiously.

"Yes, thank you," she assured him.

Turri gave her the rose wrapped in a piece of damask cloth. Carlotta unwrapped the cloth and took the rose. Inhaling its scent, "How romantic of you," she told him pleased. "And why did you wrap it in a piece of damask?" she asked.

"Carlotta, you're going to laugh at me for this," Turri shyly began telling her. "Anyway this morning while I was following the butler on my way to see you I noticed that the sumptuous salons were full of masterpieces. Besides I saw the hall of flags full of standards, banners, flags which your valiant ancestors brought back from the battlefields from Lepanto to Vienna, all through the centuries. My ancestors also fought and died at Lepanto and were at the defense of Vienna but history didn't record their names. They were small fry, good only to fight and die under those flags that adorn your salons. Therefore at home we don't have any of them. We don't have masterpieces either, only penny lithographs."

"Turri, what's the point?" she asked somewhat bored.

"The point is that I wanted to bring you something valuable, on a par with your art treasures. The most precious thing I could give you was this piece of red and gold damask. It's a part of the Bourbon flag captured by the Thousand at the battle of Calatafimi. The Bourbon army under Landi besides being ten times more numerous and better armed than the thousand plus a handful of local patriots under Garibaldi was placed on the hilltop. The patriots down the valley were an easy target for the Bourbons and mowed them down while attempting to capture the hill. Among the braves climbing the bloody hill was Turri di Motia, my maternal grandfather, who was sixteen years old then. Late that afternoon the volunteers were near disaster. However at sunset they had captured the hill, having beaten the hell out of the, Bourbon army. My grandfather had disobeyed his father and had joined the Garibaldine forces from the day of their landing from two ships at Marsala to the last battle fought at the Volturno River practically reuniting all of Italy. Afterwards my grandfather returned home penniless and an unsung hero, with only this bit of flag a memento of the Battle of Calatafimi in his pocket. He lived the rest of his life peaceably. He died when I was eight years old. On his death-bed he called for me. He gave me this bit of flag. "Take it," he told me in a feeble voice. "It represents my efforts toward the unification of Italy. My son, I wish you would pair it with another bit of flag representing your own efforts toward the unification of Europe," and he left the world.

"And do you give me this relic so dear to you? What am I going to do with this piece of trash?" she thought disgusted.

"Yes. It means a lot to me but I give it gladly to you, my love, to cover with it a small part of my immense shame for coming to this rendezvous in secrecy and by night like a criminal."

"The squirt's got a lot of pride!" the princess thought. She had a mind to kick him out, but decided to have a little fun with him first. She hugged Turri and holding him tightly to her bosom she kissed him. "I chose to let you in by night not to cover your worthlessness but to protect our love from the world's shallow understanding of the heart's deep emotions. Come!" she said taking him by the hand and gently dragging him through the walk and up the stairs. "Caspita! Turri doesn't grasp the ephemeral nature of our fling, that like a page torn from a book and carried by the wind, has neither a past nor a future. I regret I deluded myself that it was possible to be sixteen years old again, even for a night. Turri has taken it for the eternal love found only in Gothic novels. It was a folly on my part to get so far involved with a child, on the other hand, who is always wise living on this foolish earth? Let the darkness cover my mistakes. Night, friend of lovers, great deceiver of human hearts, foster in me this illusion of being an adolescent, again in at least until dawn or perhaps until I meet a man with means, who will keep me at my life-style's level above that of the pretentious Madames Bovaries of my time. Does Turri, understand my predicament? I need a rich redeemer not a penniless lover-boy now that the Salinas fortune is almost gone. I can't count on my father who gambles away what we have left, nor on my brother, Philip, who instead of trying to marry into money is engaged to Ann Nascone, a totally penniless bitch."

Hand in hand, Carlotta and Turri crossed the corridor making the least possible noise and stopped at the door of what Turri thought was Carlotta's bedroom. For a few seconds they hugged and kissed each other in the dark after entering the room.

If the prince, your father, or your brother found me like this with you they'd kill me. I wouldn't mind dying in your arms, though."

"Caspita! Caspita to the n-th power!" Carlotta almost cried out loud. "Did I talk like him when I was eighteen? Or is he more immature than I thought?" However, she thought it was too late for her to alter her plans and she went along with them for the bit of fun she expected to get out of this. When she turned the lights on Turri noticed it wasn't her bedroom. Carlotta explained that indeed it was her parents bedroom. However, nobody would come and disturb them because her father hadn't entered it in sixteen years and he had forbidden anyone to go in except the cleaning woman.

"For sixteen years, eh?" Turri commented. "Since your mother died, I guess."

My mother didn't die. She ran away with Ross Gevaert, a rich American industrialist, leaving behind my father, my younger brother Philip, and me. She and Ross live in Boston."

Turri glanced at the room's old fashioned decor and at its piece de resistance, the Empire bed covered by a pale-blue chenille. His main attention was focused on Carlotta. In the darkness he had surmised what she wore. Now he could see it clearly in the bright light of a dozen miniature chandeliers hanging from the frescoed ceiling. Carlotta was wearing a simple chemise of black tulle adorned by a narrow silver belt. "She is a classy lady of exquisite taste," Turri commented to himself. As it would have been beneath her to pretend she went straight to the point. She turned the lights off except for one and began to undress. When she shed every garment Turri stared at her harmonious body as a masterpiece come out of the hands of the most refined artist. "Carlotta! You are the most beautiful woman on earth," he cried full of admiration and passion. He had seen her lovely body before and had touched its silky texture, and had inhaled its natural scent mixed with that of verbena. He had done so by fortuitous circumstances. It was a different situation now. She was ready to give herself freely to him. It would be the most precious gift he would ever receive as long as he lived. Turri was accepting it in the name of love and he would never question her motive. He only knew that she was about to make him the happiest man on earth. That was all that mattered to him now. The future was beyond the power of his personal influence. The universal power that had arranged to bring them together would also spin the rest of the fairy tale and he and Carlotta would live together and happily ever after. "Carlotta!" he called her.

"God, his big mouth's open again. Will he ever stop talking nonsense," Carlotta complained vexed. "Yes, Turri, What is it?"

"You give me love, beauty, class, style, and what not. What shall I give you in return?"

"You don't have to give me anything. Just shut up!"

"I remember the first time I saw you, in the foyer of the Teatro Massimo at the performance of Aida. Radames, as I recall, sang that he wanted to give Aida, a throne near the sun. I wish I could give you that throne. You deserve it."

"Stop talking, undress and join me here in bed or is the water too cold for you?" she teased him while stretching herself provocatively on the pale-blue linen. Turri didn't need any coaxing to join her and found the water temperature perfect for the plunge. That symbolic water she had just mentioned would serve for his baptism of love administered to him by the young priestess, exquisitely beautiful, with velvety black hair, emerald eyes, a Greek goddess's bust, long perfect legs, and the lovely harmonious rest. He himself didn't make a bad impression on her. She saw him radiantly handsome standing near her with his youthful strength softened by the invisible halo of innocence.

Tonight's experience will hardly scratch away his innocence. He has a pure soul which all the grime of life won't succeed in soiling," Carlotta commented to herself. "I seduced him and he believes he has seduced me. That's not all. Our souls are of two different kinds and they never will blend together. This affair will remain a pleasant memory, a flower squeezed between the dull pages of our lives, and no more." Carlotta crouched and assumed a sitting position. "Come to me!" she called invitingly with open arms. Turri ran to her and kneeled by the bed. She closed her arms around his neck and he kissed the light-brown hard and small nipples of her round, perfect breasts. Carlotta drew him into bed with her and they reclined together. They played caressed, and kissed for a while then she let him part her legs. With imperceptible diligent movements she guided and received the neophyte. Commotion, fugue, and ecstasy followed. When the storm subsided Turri rolled over. In the agony of the aftermath he realized he had joined the world of grown ups at the price of a lost privacy of body and a contaminated soul. For a while he thought he had reached the highest heaven when indeed he had his feet deeper on earth. The kind of love he felt for Carlotta tied him stronger to this planet full of evil. Soon the goddess who just a few seconds ago had filled his cup with nectar now she was pouring venom into it. "My dear, it's time for you to leave. Your parents undoubtedly are anxiously waiting for you," the sweet Carlotta of few moments ago lashed at him "Do you want me to leave so soon?" Turri asked dejected.

"It's because I don't want your parents to worry

about you. It's late you know. It's two o'clock in the morning."

"I only have my mother and she's not waiting for me," Turri argued trying to remain a little longer with her.

"Then it's even worse than I thought. I'm sure she will worry until you get back home. Please go!" Carlotta got up and put on a purple chiffon negligee, then she helped Turri put his clothes back on. No sooner was Turri dressed than Carlotta accompanied him to the veranda.

Turri couldn't understand her quick change of mood. "Why does she act this way?" he thought in anguish. "Is it because she detected that somebody has discovered us or she doesn't love me anymore because I disappointed her?" For whatever reason she was pushing him out. Before leaving, with one foot on the first step of the staircase Turri turned his head and asked anxiously, "Is it all over between us or will you permit me to come to see you again?" Carlotta ruffled the kid's hair and with a reassuring smile whispered into his ear, "Blockhead, it's not over between us. Come back here to-morrow night at the same hour."

Turri gratefully kissed her hand and quickly disappeared in the darkness of the gardens. His heart was full of joy. He basked in the illusion of having found in her the love he had always dreamed of that lasts a lifetime and beyond.

In a week's time Turri managed to sleep with Carlotta three full nights. His success made him grow too possessive toward her while she grew annoyed of him and his interminable talk. "You are my share of carnal and romantic love," he blurted out one night. "From the time I was this high I have dreamed of obtaining my fair share of every good thing under the sun. My fair share of love, joy, health, my fair share of land, ocean, sky. My fair share of bread and dwelling, my fair share of talent, glory; my fair share of Heaven and everything else."

"What about your fair share of suffering? Will you claim that also or do you only want the goodies?" Carlotta teased him.

I will accept my share of suffering in every form except one, that of losing you. I couldn't bear it. As a matter of fact, I would willingly trade off all the other shares that destiny owes me for the share of your love. I have been invaded by your loveliness. You have enriched my life and you've also taken a few things from it. As a result of it I an not free, am not whole, I am not rational away from you. You are my cross and also, my source of ineffable joy; you are both, the despair of my body and its consolation, the tempestuous ocean foundering my wandering spirit and also its port of rest. Away from you I have no peace. I need you. Please tell me that you will be mine forever!" he besought Carlotta unashamedly.

"I'll be yours forever," she lied. She couldn't bring herself to tell him that it was all over between them. Carlotta had found the lover she had been looking for. His name was Tonio Giaccone. Tonio had ideas in his mind more outrageous than Turri's. However he was the sole heir of the rich widow Giaccone. Carlotta didn't care much for Tonio, but she would willingly marry him for the great fortune he would inherit from his grandmother. If all went according to her plan she could become the richest woman in Europe, thus she could pay her father's enormous debts and also restore the lost splendor of the Salinas House and the Leopard would glitter again. Under the circumstances Carlotta felt it would be more than gracious to allow Turri one last encounter. She would tell him the last lie.

When Wednesday night came, Turri opened Villa Augusta's back gate and proceeded through the walk flanked by tall palm-trees toward the veranda. It was a cloudy night, but Turri by now could have found his way blind-folded. A fierce Maestrale wind was slapping his face and bending the palm-trees somewhat. When he reached the veranda, Carlotta wasn't there waiting for him. "In weather like this I don't blame her for staying indoors," he thought. Turri crossed the corridor and stopped in front of the well known bedroom door. He knocked on it gently. Carlotta opened the door and let him in. To his surprise she was smoking a Macedonia through a long ebony cigarette-holder. She was wearing a spring-green colored chiffon negligee with ribbons of white satin held together by three small clasps of agate. To his eyes she was more beautiful than ever, but somehow much different. She wore more make-up than ever, and her verbena, scent had been supplanted by a much richer and provocative perfume. They said hello without hugging or kissing each other. Turri didn't want to touch her with his cold hands, and she didn't want to be touched, he thought with anguish. He noticed that the porphyry ash-tray was full of Macedonia butts. She hadn't smoked once when they had been together and he thought she didn't smoke. Now there was enough evidence in front of him showing that Carlotta was a chain-smoker. The room was saturated with smoke and she kept adding to it by lighting another Macedonia and letting the smoke rise in small rings. "She's a tobacco addict and a virtuoso," Turri thought, with consternation Carlotta, poured hot coffee from a golden coffee pot into two Meissen demi-tasses. She gave one to Turri and took the other for herself, then both went to sit in the comfortable sofa. "I didn't know you smoked," Turri told her showing surprise.

"It's one of my many facets that you didn't know of. I live a complex adult life. When I am with you I go back to the age of innocence, in a world a la Paul et Virginie," she told him with a pungent sarcasm.

"Does it mean that you have been playing a child's game with me?" Turri asked disheartened.

"No. Never," she lied to him. "It's only that I regret that I'll have to abandon, for a short while, our Eden of innocence and ought to go back into the wicked world of adulthood." I'm tired of this make-believe.

"Are you telling me this is the end of our relationship?" Turri asked sadly.

"No, it isn't" she answered him smilingly after having blown another cloud of smoke into his face. "It's just that my father and a few of my close friends suspect that I don't spend all these nights at home by myself reading Holy Writ or the Lives of the Saints. Therefore I'll have to resume my public life for awhile."

"For a while. How long is a while?"

"A few days. Till the coast is clear again. It won't take me long to bury the truth in a few lies," she added throwing another puff of smoke into his face that made him cough.

"Drink your coffee! It's getting cold," she scolded him.

"Who cares if the coffee gets cold? I don't. If

it gets icy I won't drink it. Anyway, even icy it won't turn into poison, it won't kill me, I only care about the temperature of the love you feel for me and it seems it's getting cold fast. I'm afraid if it gets colder it will turn into ice. If this should ever happen it would turn into the most deadly poison for me and would kill me instantly."

"Do I have to listen to this childish, romantic rubbish?" Carlotta thought disgusted, "Shouldn't I throw him out right now?" She calmed down and was more indulgent with Turri, opting to let him rant at will. "After all, it's the last time he has a chance to do it, as I won't allow him to set foot in here again," she thought with relief. "If he had only kept his big mouth shut we could have enjoyed this last encounter. I'll salvage what I can," she decided. "I am doing it to protect our relationship, to keep it secret," she explained.

"For how long has our relationship yet to be kept secret? Will the time ever come when you will reveal it to the world?" he anxiously asked.

"Be patient a while longer my dearest. The right time will come," she assured him. Turning-toward the commode to reach the silver cigarette-case on top of it somehow made her negligee fall open. Turri stared at her voluptuous nakedness. Carlotta noticed his eager desire. "Toujours des perdrix! Will you, ever be sated?" she asked with sarcasm.

"Never!" he answered.

"You will," she remarked getting up and going to put her empty demi-tasse back in the tray. Then she turned the lights off except, one, and began to undress. She reclined in bed.

"Come here, child," she called invitingly. Turri didn't know what to do. He had a confused mind and an aching heart. It was clear to him that Carlotta didn't love him anymore but charitably she was giving herself to him for the last time. He was deeply hurt and didn't want any alms of love from her. He wanted to tell Carlotta he knew that her words were all lies, and yet he felt, "Beautiful liar." "Come!" she called again. Turri surrendered at the sweet sound of her voice and docile like the most servile slave he obeyed the command of his mistress. His agonizing thoughts and pains vanished when she was holding him in her arms and in the following delirium of love-making. "God, let this night last forever I beseech you!" he prayed, but dawn came swiftly. "God, you didn't hear my prayer. You didn't bother to answer an ass like me. I'm damned." Soon it was time for him to leave Carlotta, his most precious jewel on earth. He put his clothes back on slowly without turning his eyes away from, her. "She throws me out of paradise although I haven't broken any commandment of love,' he commented broken-hearted. Carlotta put on her negligee and accompanied Turri to the veranda. There he kissed her again and again. "When shall I see you again?" he asked in anguish with a foot on the first step of the staircase.

"I'll call you when it's time," she said unconvincingly. Turri walked slowly to his exile wanting to believe in the sincerely of her words. It took him a long time to reach the back gate. He got there short of breath as if he had crossed the length of the Sahara desert. He opened the gate and stepped into the bleak world of suffering human beings like himself. Like Dante, I know now that I have been thrown out of the dwelling of my loved one and how you felt being exiled from your beloved Florence and away from Beatrice," he raved.

Will I also die at Ravenna or will the beautiful and cruel harlot permit me to return here and die at her feet?"

Turri turned his head once more toward Villa Augusta before boarding the bus.

"Please let me off at Florence," he told the middle-aged sleepy bus-driver.

"Sure, son." The driver answered thinking the young man was inebriated. We will get there like in the Greek legends."

Chapter IX

On St. John's day early in the morning the heat had become more unbearable yet. Even in the murderous hot weather flocks of pilgrims had rushed to consult the Sibyl. Before descending into the grotto they circled the level ground chapel with its walls in ruins and a fallen roof, thirteen times. Exhausted and staggering under the hot sun they continued circling the chapel while some of them either dropped out or fainted. The majority of the pilgrims were women past their prime with evident afflictions of the flesh and less evident spiritual ones. Their expressions showed resignation to the baffling cause of their innocent suffering. Some of them had dragged their young and pretty daughters along. They had little to ask the Sibyl and little hope for themselves. They came to know mainly what the future held for their children, wishing it would be better than their own. The girls couldn't have cared less. They had their minds and eyes set on the boys. Their future depended on the reaction they'd get from them and tried to display their charms in the best way possible through their gauzy transparent dresses cut very short. The young men in flannel suits observed what the girls were offering them and were eager to feel the quality of their charms but they didn't bother asking for the Sibyl's guidance on the matter. Among the throng of pilgrims circling the chapel were Elvira and her son Tonio. At forty-six, although heavier than in her youth, she had kept the attributes of the beautiful blondes of the North. Turri, on the contrary, although he inherited his mother's features, was dark skinned as if tanned by the Southern sun. Elvira spotted Marietta Burruni among the throng. She was getting close to them. Marietta was a notorious whore and a pretty brunette in her early thirties, who lived on the Striscia border. She was disliked by everyone except her local customers and out of town sailors.

"What is she doing here?" Elvira asked Tonio. "This is not the place for her to be."

"Mother, she's, in the right place and with the right crowd of blockheads. The question is what are we doing here among them?"

"You know as well as I do that she shouldn't be here, but I won't argue with you in weather like this. That the kids are behaving shamefully, pinching the girls derrieres et cetera, has made it a bad moral environment already. Now she shows up. Will she practice her trade out here or down there turning this holy shrine into an infernal bulge?"

"Mother, I'm surprised at you. This is an unusual display of lack of sympathy toward your fellowmen. Fellow women, I mean. Let's go home, please! Doing so we will avoid witnessing whatever Marietta plans to do."

"No. We will go home after we have accomplished what we came here for and not a minute sooner. I won't let Marietta thwart our purpose," Elvira replied. "And you know what? Its time for you to get down the grotto and ask the Sibyl about your destiny; whether you will live long, be rich, famous; whether you will marry and whom," she whispered into his ear. "Go now! I'll wait for you here." Tonio made his last effort of resistance, "Mother, please, don't make me go down there. You know as well as I do that the Sibyl oracles and the Orphic doctrine are more than ludicrous, nowadays. Persephone hasn't picked narcissi in the Enna's gardens in the last twenty centuries. Why do you insist on our making fools of ourselves?"

"Turri, my son, you don't know everything. Even then if you lacked wisdom your knowledge would be of no avail to you. You perceive, as well as I do, that around us nothing lasts but all perishes. Therefore we need to take a glimpse at our future somehow. The Sibyl affords us that glimpse. I need to know before I die what's going to happen to you. Don't deny me this opportunity! Go down there for my sake. I went to the grotto myself when I was a girl and asked the Sibyl for my oracle. It foresaw that I was going to become a fisherman's wife. What a blow that was to me. How could I live with an ignoramus? I had to say good-bye to my dreams and hopes, to the tinsel and glitter of cultural refinement. It proved to be a worse disappointment than I had suspected. I don't have to tell you that your father had a handsome body—but his soul was and is that of an ass. There was a time when I loved the spacious and loquacious sea. Because of your father I now detest it. I married a fisherman when I had hoped to marry a prince, an author or an artist," she sighed.

"Mother, you shouldn't have come here in the first place, and moreover you should have disregarded the Sibyl's oracle as the nonsense that it is."

Turri saw his mother growing pale. She hadn't felt very well lately. He thought he had aggravated her illness by not pleasing her. As soon as Elvira felt better Tonio headed for the grotto. He descended the roughly hewn steps that led to the mossy and humid cave. It seemed to him the grotto was an ancient dungeon, and the well of fresh water at its center attested to it as an old cistern. On his left Tonio saw an alcove dug out, of the rock. "It's the Sibyl's bed," someone in the crowd commented aloud. Tonio followed the crowd and when he reached the alcove he stopped in front of it. Facing the alcove he followed his mother's instructions.

"Divine Sibyl," he asked in jest, "tell me whom shall I marry?" He didn't expect any answer and there was, none. He repeated the question. No answer either. He heard the noise of the bustling crowd. Turri asked the question for the third time. He only heard Marietta Burruni commenting out loud, "You mean to tell me he will marry a princess? That's great!"

"That couldn't be taken for the Sibyl's oracle," he said to himself and ascended the slippery steps to rejoin his mother. As soon as Elvira saw Tonio in front of the grotto she ran to meet him.

"Tonio, what did the oracle say?" she asked him anxiously.

"It said that I will marry Marietta Burruni," he told her in jest. No sooner had Elvira heard Marietta's, name than she fainted into Tonio's arms. "With my bad taste joke I've killed my own mother," Tonio cried. "Mother, I was kidding you!" he kept shouting in despair. "I'm sorry. I shouldn't have done it." With great care and in tears he succeeded in reviving her.

"Did you say you were only kidding me?" Elvira asked as soon as she regained her consciousness.

"Yes, mother. I'm sorry."

"Let me hear the oracle, then."

"It's such nonsense that we should forget about it," Tonio answered, reluctant to give credence to the humbug by repeating it.

"I want to hear it. Tell me?" she pleaded.

"I heard Marietta Burruni after I asked the Sibyl, 'Who will I marry?' saying, 'a princess? That's great!' Anyway, who does pay attention to what Marietta says?"

"My son, you brought me best news ever. Those words that you heard weren't Marietta Burruni's, they were the words the Sibyl spoke to you through Marietta's lips," Eivira jubilantly explained to him falling on her knees, "I thank you, merciful God," she prayed, "for letting my Turri marry a princess."

"Holy smokes, my mother's making a big deal out of this nonsense!" Tonio commented with great concern. "Mother, since when did Marietta's words become divine oracles?" Tonio asked incredulously.

"My son, please, it's good news, wonderful news. Don't spoil it for me! Help me individuate who's the princess you are going to marry!"

"Mother, hold your horses."

Elvira didn't hear him. "Let me see. Princess Amelia isn't in her prime. It can't be her. Princess Carolina hasn't a thing worthy to pinch, and it can't be her, either. Princess Carlotta Salinas is your age, and she's beautiful and you have been together before. She's the one. Princess Carlotta Salinas is your future wife," Elvira concluded happily.

"Mother, don't spread this nonsense around or I'll be the town laughing stock," Tonio pleaded.

"But it's true. The oracle said so."

"Mother, this oracle's becoming a problem already."

"No, don't say that. The only problem's your father. What are we going to do with him? He's so uncouth. He's out of place even in our home, imagine how much more so he'd be at Villa Augusta!"

"Mother, none of us will ever even set foot at Villa Augusta to be formally introduced to Prince Salinas and his daughter, Princess Carlotta. There is no reason to denigrate my father. We know he's an ass, but if we, his own loved ones, despise him, who else will love him?" Tonio cried.

"Don't worry about that," Elvira told her son, "he's loved by his four brothers, his three sisters and by half a billion relatives. They are as numerous as ants in an anthill. If that isn't enough he's also loved by all the wet-bottoms like him that infest that dump-site they call the Striscia," said Elvira. Then she added, "Of course all his tacky relatives won't be invited to your wedding. I wish

I could find a way to also bar your father. That way we'll keep the jungle out of the Villa . With God's help your wedding will be a magnificent one."

"Mother, you keep talking of my wedding to Princess Salinas as if it were real rather than imaginary. Calm yourself down, please. Don't get carried away by your fervid imagination! Princess Carlotta Salinas wouldn't get near me again if we were marooned on a desert island and we were the only inhabitants. I can't imagine that she would marry me here where she has the entire cream of society to choose from for her husband. We're by no means in the same league," argued Tonio, exasperated at his mother's flight from reality.

"Do you think you're unworthy of marrying a princess? Is that what's bothering you?" asked Elvira.

"Yes, among other things," Tonio answered.

"Then it's time for me to let you in on a family secret. The fact is that in your arteries royal blood runs."

"Mother, are you feeling all right? Or is this a delirium talk caused by a high fever?" asked Tonio, alarmed.

"No, my son. I'm all right. What I've told you is the gospel truth. In your veins runs illegitimate royal blood, but royal just the same. My great grandmother Eloisa Damiani, God bless her soul, was the illegitimate daughter of King Ferdinand II of Bourbon. You are the great grandson of a king, and worthy of marrying a princess," Elvira concluded.

"Mother, has rationality left you? Do you really expect me to go to Villa Augusta and appear before Prince Salinas and tell him, "Prince, let me introduce myself. I am Tonio Giaccone, a college professor . I have not a penny to my name, but I am an illegitimate great grandson of king Ferdinand II. I want to marry your daughter on account that Marietta Burruni said so."

"No, not Marietta Burruni, but the Sibyl said so," Elvira corrected Tonio, annoyed by his skeptical attitude.

"Just the same, who would blame the princess if she mistook me for a clown and in an uproar told the servants to throw me out via the back staircase? Mother, dear. I am sorry but I can't do that, even for your sake," Tonio said firmly. Mother and son started an argument that lasted all the way home. Elvira refuted every objection that Tonio could think of. "You don't have to go to Villa Augusta until the time comes. Lately I have seen you with Baron Armando Amadeo, your schoolmate. He's a relative of Princess Salinas, isn't he?"

"Yes, he is," Tonio answered guessing his mother's scheme. Baron Amadeo, a friend of his since the Liceo was also his roommate at the university. They hadn't seen much of each other lately, though.

"Mother, don't tell me you plan to use Armando as an intermediary. It won't work that way either."

"I'll handle it," Elvira said confidently.

No sooner was she back home than she called Armando Amadeo. Two days later Tonio stood in front of Villa Bordighera, for a while contemplating the building and its gardens. It was a visit to a familiar place for him. He hadn't been there since his Liceo days when the young baron used to invite him often to spend a weekend with him. Tonio noticed that few changes had taken place since the last time he was there. The building showed scars from neglected maintenance, and the gardens, had made incipient inroads, so that wilderness surrounded them. The villa was one of the few pieces of real estate left to the Amadeos. Turri didn't have the occasion to say hello to Baron and Baroness Amadeo as they were away on a Greek Islands cruise continuing to squander whatever remained of their once great fortune. They were going down the drain, but in style. Armando, chip off the same block, saw disaster approaching but didn't bother to alter its course either. He could find employment as source of another income, but the thought of going to work never entered the antechamber of his mind. His interests lay in perfecting his tennis game and in diving. If the worse came to the worst, and it was very closely approaching, he would marry Maria Luisa Giarratano. She was the only child of Pasquale Giarratano, the rich wine-maker who wanted to pin a title on his Maria Luisa. It wasn't the usual case of an ugly and uncouth daughter of the nouveaux riches trying to marry herself to a nobleman in need of cash that she would bring him. Only the second circumstance was true here, because Maria Luisa was a beautiful twenty-one year old, intelligent, and college educated brunette. On the other hand, Baron Amadeo, it was not a secret, needed her money. However, people believed that if half of the usual occurrence was true the other half had, to be true, also. Otherwise, they reasoned, how would she, also beautiful, so rich, and well educated, consent to marry a not-so-hot looking and penniless baron? As Maria didn't possess any overt physical defects they thought she must have a hidden one, a mental flaw.

The rumor went about that Maria Luisa was a loony and had spent time locked in nut-houses in places so secret that only the very rich could afford. But her neighbors hadn't noticed any abnormal activities, nor had they heard any screaming in the middle of the night, nor anything else usually associated with madness, coming out of the Giarratano's mansion, except the usual cursing aloud and the litany of profanities broadcast to the entire world by Mr. Giarratano whenever he was angry. That is to say, often. That false, and ugly rumor started the moment the news of Armando and Maria Luisa's engagement had been made public. At first Armando didn't believe the rumor had any foundation and he discarded it as a base calumny. However, as the days and weeks went by and the rumor still persisted, he wavered and began scrutinizing Maria Luisa's behavior trying to detect any abnormalities in it. "Where there is smoke, there is fire after all," he believed, and began his investigation with such a prejudicial premise. As an amateur clinical observer Armando was a flop. Maria Luisa found him hiding in her bedroom closet, in the pantry, in the stable loft, and, more than once in the back-seat of her green Citroen. Besides, he stared at her in such a way that she became suspicious that he was mentally deranged. Armando had never attempted to harm her, but, who knows? "Fits of madness are unpredictable," she thought, and if a violent one seized him he might, kill her. Therefore, Maria Luisa was always en garde in his presence. She never contradicted Armando. She always smiled at him, and always located herself near doors for a quick escape, if needs be. On the other hand, her fake smiles, her furtive manners, her constant unreasonable fear of him, confirmed Armando's suspicions about Maria Luisa. He postponed their wedding date, hoping she'd have such an open fit of madness, not in his presence, he prayed, that she would be required to be locked in a nut-house for a very long time and the wedding would be called off. "I don't want to marry that crazy broad. To hell with her money! She'd drive me crazy and I don't want to be locked in a nut-house for life myself. No, siree!"

Turri and Armando greeted each other and took a walk in the park.

"All women are crazy!" cried Armando.

"Maria Luisa included?" Tonio asked facetiously.

"How do you know she's crazy?" asked Armando surprised.

"There is this rumor going around," said Tonio apologetically. Is there any truth in it?"

"Unfortunately, yes. Don't tell anyone if I tell you that she is as loony as Ophelia. In my opinion all women are crazy in various degrees. Except Princess Carlotta, of course. She has her faults, but she is not crazy. You're a lucky man, my friend, to be marrying her," he told Tonio.

"What did you say?" asked Tonio, surprised by Armando matter of fact remark.

"I said that you're a lucky man to marry princess Carlotta Salinas. She's not crazy like the others."

"Does it mean that you already told the princess that stupid prophecy of the Sibyl?" asked Tonio mortified.

"Yes, of course. As soon as your mother told me about the prophecy, that day I ran to Villa Augusta and told the good news to the person most entitled to know all about it. Do you disapprove?"

"Yes, I do. As a matter of fact, I came here for the sole purpose of asking you, if you hadn't already done so, not to tell the princess. You know as well as I do that the Sibyl's oracle is nonsense. As I have come here too late to prevent it, will you do me the great favor of going to convince the princess to forgive my mother's credulity," Tonio implored. "Add, also, to accept my apology for having her name dragged into such a shameful incident."

"Tonio, take heart! There's no need of an apology. Princess Carlotta was absolutely thrilled by the prophecy. As a matter of fact she's eager to see you, the man destiny has given her as her beloved husband in such an arcane way, She told me to invite you on her behalf to Villa Augusta for next Wednesday night. She's giving a party in your honor. She's so eager to introduce you to her friends and relatives. Be there, please!" Armando implored. "Don't disappoint the princess!"

"No. I absolutely can't come," Tonio replied.

"Please, don't say no to such a lovely woman," Armando cajoled.

"I'd like very much to come and meet the princess," said Tonio, "but not under the auspices of the Sibyl's prophecy. Why should we play this farce, poking fun at a populace's superstition and hurting somebody's feelings in the process, mainly my mother's and mine? Couldn't I meet Princess Salinas in a serious normal way?" asked Tonio.

"This is a normal way," replied Armando. "As I said earlier, the party gives the princess the opportunity to make it publicly known that she's going to marry you."

Armando, you can't be serious! Are you telling me the princess has actually made up her mind to marry me solely on the basis of the Sibyl's prophecy?" asked Tonio, incredulously.

"She knows what kind of a person you are. I more than adequately filled in the blank spaces for her as I know you very well. Besides, as I said before, she's, thrilled by the whole thing. Though it's true that her father is less than enthusiastic about it, he'll come around. There's nothing for you to fear. Be there!" Armando injected with a lot of enthusiasm. "We'll revel a little, of course, in the old Dionysian way. What's wrong with that? After all, we are children at heart and we are thrilled by mystery, prophecies, ancient beliefs, and arcane rituals. In our eyes you and your mother are not objects of ridicule but rather of sincere appreciation for the revival of the Orphic mysteries. As a matter of fact, there is now a fervor in many of us to restore the old temples at Acragas, Seline, Segesta, etc., and to go back to living the simple life of ancient times. Shall I tell the princess that you will oblige her by coming?" Armando asked in a mockingly suppliant posture.

"I don't know," answered Tonio, wavering. "Do you want me to play the clown for the princess's amusement? Well, so be it, then," he said with a sigh of resignation.

Armando was jubilant. He forced Tonio into having a large and rather heavy dinner with him on the veranda.

As soon as Tonio left Villa Bordighera, Armando telephoned princess Carlotta. "Tonio just left," he began telling her. "Before leaving he promised to come to the party Wednesday evening. It took me a great deal of effort to extract that promise from him. You could have done it easily, I know that, but he's not such a dummy as you think, my dear princess. As a matter of fact he knows exactly what to expect when he gets to

Villa Augusta. I ask you again to reconsider your plan. It's too harsh. Why do you want to hurt the dear fellow? You have your reasons. Anyway I'm betraying an old friend. I've thought all along that there must be a better way for us to grab away his grandmother's immense fortune. I found out it's in the neighborhood of two trillion lire. Mamma mia! That much. I don't think the old witch knows how much that is. Anyway, you practically have Turri Giaccone in the palm of your hand right now. Why do you insist on humiliating him? He's a sensitive soul and if you hurt him badly in public I'm afraid that you'll be killing the very goose that will lay the golden eggs. Yes, Princess, I should mind my own business, but don't forget that you have a rival. Yes. Her name is Paluzza Oliveri. She hasn't given up on him. She shadows him wherever he goes. She followed him here! I must say what a beautiful lass! No, she is not more beautiful than you, princess. I apologize. I didn't mean nor did I imply that." "What a vain broad!" he muttered in his thoughts.

"Yes, Paluzza stood in front of my gate while Tonio was visiting with me. Why do I bore you with such trite gossip? Because I thought you should know about this stubborn girl. Tonio might open his eyes some day and see how beautiful she is. He would run back to her, then. Yes, I will shut up. As for the rest of the plan—things are running smoothly. I paid Marietta Burruni the 5,000 lire we agreed upon, and from my own pocket, against the eventual 10% of your gross. You're tired, I understand. Good-night, princess. I'll see you Wednesday evening!" Armando came out of that conversation with Princess Carlotta Salinas very irritated. "She's so beautiful but also such a bitch" he exploded, venting his bile. "Beauty, for sure, is in the eye of the beholder, after all. Paluzza,in my eyes is the most beautiful blonde I have ever seen, while Tonio doesn't see much in her. He prefers someone else. If it were up, to me, and I didn't need the money, I'd marry Paluzza tomorrow, if she wanted me, rather than Maria Luisa, that loony. I'd better give that dumb broad a call to tell her to get ready for Wednesday night."

Chapter X

Wednesday evening Tonio arrived at Villa Augusta in his shiny but ancient Fiat Balilla. A valet came to park the car and he crossed the vast marble-paved portico of the immense green domed palace.

"A replica of Versailles maybe?" he commented. It was a magnificent artifact, beautiful, but passé, but who wants to live there?" he asked himself. He looked around pleased by the view of the formal French gardens, the fountains, the courtyard with a series of colonnaded outhouses, and the other side of the palace's magnificent park, Tonio entered the ornate vestibule and there, waiting for him, was Armando. He guided Tonio into the main oval-shaped ballroom. On its ceiling there was a Valeriani fresco of Diana leaving for the deer-chase.

"Baroque at the apogee of its splendor," Tonio commented. He admired the profusion of paintings, stucco frescoes, mirrors, chandeliers, all very ornate—too ornate. The guests and the atmosphere were all of yesterday. When in a short while he saw Princess Carlotta descending the marble-staircase in a purple satin gown, making quite a theatrical entrance in her plumaged hairdo, Turri knew he was expected to play the buffoon as he had anticipated. Realizing it was too late for him to retreat he decided improvise his role. Evidently the princess's appearance meant that the curtain was drawn and that the comedy could begin to be played. Obviously the guests were already familiar with the plot that was to unfold. No sooner had they seen the princess coming down the stairs than they were all gathered around Tonio. He knew he had to play his part whether he liked it or not. Armando promised this wouldn't happen. I figure her excellency will try to amuse her guests with witty tirades. I'm certain she will pretend to be under the Sibyl's spell and will immediately fake falling madly in love with me. She's looking for her victim. You won't miss your target, Princess. Armando is pushing me toward the foot of the staircase," he grumbled. No sooner had her eyes met Tonio's than Carlotta ran toward him, holding up the hem of her gown so that she wouldn't trip in her haste. Faking a torrid passion, she hugged and kissed him. In a nasal cultivated voice she sighed, "My love, at last you're in my arms and I in yours. Hold me tightly to your bosom, love of my destiny. Without you, there has been such an emptiness, in my life. Now I can't live without you!"

Her friends applauded her well spoken lines. Indeed, she was playing her part beautifully. On the other hand Tonio was in a very awkward situation. While he was delighted holding this extremely voluptuous woman, whose scent was inebriating all of his senses, he also was outraged by her motive to mock him. Besides, those damn feathers of her headdress were penetrating his nostrils and poking into his eyes. With one hand he tried to push the feathers away, while with the other hand, he held the princess tightly to him and without stopping kissed those silky and luscious lips of hers. She tried to disengage herself from the brute but he held onto her firmly. Playing his part by ear he told her loudly, "Princess, my true and only love, holding you in my arms makes me the happiest man on earth. This is the most wonderful and splendid day of my life. Finally destiny has brought us together and we will spend the rest of our lives together. What bliss this is!"

"I am Tonio Giaccone, as your excellency has rightly guessed," he whispered into her ear. "I am absolutely delighted. About, this play…we really should have rehearsed our parts. To tell you the truth, I'm not very good at improvisations."

His words made the princess's blood pressure abruptly rise, but she didn't lose her composure. She realized that he wasn't a clod. This notion made the intended unfolding of her plot impossible. She immediately abandoned it and lead Turri by the hand, away from the crowd. They walked through a corridor and entered the first unoccupied chamber. She closed the ornate door behind them.

"It's evident that you don't believe in the Sibyl's prophecy at all. Why have you come here, then? she asked him while hardly controlling her rage.

"I've come here solely for the great privilege of meeting you formally, princess. Hasn't. Armando told you about any of this?" he said apologetically, as if she were the victim of his joke.

"Perhaps he did, but who pays attention to what Armando says?" she remarked contemptuously.

"'Then I exceeded your expectations. You wanted a total idiot to show up so that you could entertain your guests. Instead I showed up, a half wit, who spoiled all of your fun. Princess Salinas, I'm terribly sorry for having caused you such trouble," he added sarcastically.

"Please stop tormenting yourself and accept my apologies for my irresponsible behavior. I was carried away by it all.

"My impertinence," he helped say the word for her.

"You wanted to get back at me, and rightly so. You saw the Sibyl's prophecy as plebeian insolence disguised as an oracle. You thought I was trying to climb the social ladder by laying my hands on your excellency. Who can blame you for wanting to teach me a lesson? I only hope you'll forgive my intrusion here. Good-bye, Princess Salinas!" Tonio kissed Carlotta's hand and rushed toward the door. He didn't, get to touch the doorknob. Carlotta prevented his departure by taking hold of his hand. "Armando was right for once," she thought. "By insisting on humiliating him I am killing the goose that will lay the golden eggs."

"Please don't go." Carlotta implored. "You insolent and proud ass," she thought resentfully,

"I'm stooping to hold your tail. Were you not made out of gold I would make leather out of your skin."

"Please, don't leave. If the Sibyl can't unite us forever, shouldn't we at least let her have her way and spend an evening together again?"

"What more do you expect from me, you fishmonger's son, to fall on my knees?" She ruminated to herself contemptuously, exasperated by his plebeian lack of flexibility.

Tonio was torn between the dictates of his heart and those of his mind. Moreover, his mind was torn between two struggling cultures. One new arid and unyielding, but, true; the other old, lush and easy, but, thick with absurdities. His heart was combining forces with the latter, whose values were dangling in the void from a line of fallacious axioms. Enthralled by the beauty of the princess, Tonio stared at her. "No, Princess, I can't stay here. To spend an evening with you is a rare opportunity and would be an immense pleasure. However my heart isn't sophisticated enough to enjoy it. What I mean is that my heart wouldn't be satisfied by spending a sole evening with you. I'm afraid that I have fallen in love with you and it's better for me not to get near you or I'll be damned forever. I have to leave. Good-bye Princess." Tonio kissed Carlotta's delicate hand and left in a hurry, leaving the princess astonished by his simultaneous declaration of love for her and sudden departure.

"Holy smoke! Am I trying to trap him or is he trying to trap me?" Carlotta asked herself. "It has become an entirely different ball-game now. I'd better go catch him. The professor's very good with words."

She followed Tonio at a distance. In the corridor she met an inquisitive Armando.

"Princess, what's happened?" I saw Tonio leaving as fast as if the devil were chasing him. Is our plan falling apart?"

"Don't worry I'll catch him," she replied.

She went into her room to change from the ball gown into more suitable attire for going out into the night and catching Tonio.

"The professor is even more of a child than Turri" she thought. "Think of it a new career is in front of me as a professional babysitter. I don't like it at all. The professor's full of shit. Fortunately, money doesn't stink, as Vespasian wisely said, even when it comes out of public urinals." She changed quickly and began her chase in the direction Armando pointed her.

Tonio drove his ancient Fiat aimlessly.

"All is vanity," he commented disgusted with himself, the princess, Armando, and the entire topsy-turvy world.

"I shouldn't have gone to Villa Augusta in the first place. I went anyway and made a complete fool of myself."

Thus absorbed, he drove down a stretch of sandy-beach. Out there the sea was gently trembling and sparkling in the pale light of the full moon.

"They say that people act crazily in full moon. At least I did!"

He parked the car at the nearest parking lot and walked toward the sea on the sand-dunes. He stopped a couple of feet away from the water and inhaled the salty breeze. The marine fragrance couldn't overcome the princess's scent still lingering on his clothes. Her scent evoked in him the real thing clinging to him, and he felt the sensation of those feathers still tickling his nostrils or blinding his eyes.

"What a stupendous woman I held in my arms, even only for a fleeting moment," he cried dejectedly.

"I've lost her forever because of my stupid pride. I couldn't have behaved with more naivete than any adolescent. Is it too late for me to go back to Villa Augusta and apologize to her? Chances are she won't let me get near her again after my juvenile and foolish declarations, of love. Lets face it, I am a jerk. Anyone else in my shoes would have gladly accepted the princess's invitation. That could have been bliss." He stooped and took a handful of sand and then let it slide off his hand.

"I'll go to my tomb empty-handed, but, with my pride intact. It's a lot of bull!"

While he was thus ruminating he saw a shapely woman approaching him. She was wrapped in a light-blue dress and a fur cape on her shoulders to shield her from the night-chill.

"It's the princess!" he cried gladly surprised. No, it can't be her. It's a figment of my feverish imagination. I've been thinking about her so intently that now I can see her vision coming to me. It's simply a trick of my wishful thinking. The real Princess Salinas wouldn't ever come near me again."

Just the same Tonio ran toward the phantom of his hallucination and hugged what he thought was empty air.

"Holy smoke! It's the princess in the flesh!" he shouted astonished in the silence of the night.

"It's me!" she confirmed in a tone of controlled rage. "What have you done to me? Why, do I find myself running after you? Have you cast a spell on me? If you have, please take it away! Is there a black magic, after all?"

"Princess, I haven't done anything," he said in dismay.

"Where did this instantaneous passion come from then? I'm so confused and so ashamed for behaving this way. The black magic's working on me, isn't it?" she asked consternated and shivering.

Tonio hugged her to shield her from the chilly marine breeze.

Princess, there is no black magic. What you feel is very human. It's passion that lets one feel and behave crazy-like. I'm in the same boat. I feel the same uncontrollable attraction toward you.

Do you want to fight it off? Try. You might be successful, who knows? I have succumbed to it myself," he said without the slightest regret.

"So have I," she said coming closer to him

and holding him tightly. They kissed, and although the beach was deserted, retired to a more remote corner. Tonio took his coat off and spread it on the sand. Carlotta reclined on it and he followed her there. They began caressing each other exploring each other's torrid body. Little by little they fell in the immemorial and primordial groove of love-making till it reached a savage and yet beautiful explosion of ecstasy which took them away from the sand, the beach, the world with its cares and miseries, and lifted them into heaven. As nothing lasts for long he soon rolled over.

"Princess, I wish this dream would last forever," Tonio said with great sadness, "that the Sibyll's prophecy were a sure event rather than a silly superstition."

"On the contrary I should say that the prophecy has been fulfilled. Aren't we here together?" Carlotta assured him. "Not only is he a clumsy lover, he also wants assurances that I'll be there when he needs me for such atrocious performances in the future."

"Then tell me so yourself with your own lips. I rely more on your word than on the Sibyl's jargon," he implored.

She thought, "It's just as I predicted. Professor, your chicken-brain works in a most predictable way."

Passing the Torch 153

She said, "I'm yours forever, cross my heart," she assured him again.

"She's joking and I'll follow suit," Tonio realized. "Crossing your heart is not enough. You have to swear by the moon that you'll be mine forever," he asked her with tongue in cheek, but seriously wished she'd meant it.

"I swear by the moon shining above that I'll be yours forever," she uttered casually. "Now, in order to fulfill my promise, help me get up and go home before I catch pneumonia out here in this chilly night," she teased him.

"Of course, my dearest princess. What a fool I am. I should have thought of it myself! I shouldn't have held you here this long and risked your health," he apologized while helping her getting up.

"Let's run to my car!" Arm in arm they hurried to the parked red Alfa Romeo. Tonio helped Carlotta into the car and saw her heading home. He followed her in his Fiat. The two cars stopped in front the huge wrought-iron gates of the Villa Augusta. Tonio alighted from the Fiat and went to Carlotta at the wheel of her Alfa Romeo. Carlotta rolled down the window.

"Do you want to come in, my love?"

"I'd better not. A few of your guests might still be there and I'm through playing the clown for tonight. When can I see you again?" Tonio implored.

"Come tomorrow evening. I'll be waiting for, you."

After a good-night kiss they parted. Tonio watched her car until it reached the main entrance plaza. Someone rushed to help her alight. Only after he saw her enter the palace did Tonio get back into his car.

It was 3 AM when Tonio got back home. His mother was dozing on the couch in the livingroom, up waiting for him. As soon as she heard his footsteps she ran to open the door for him. He had barely crossed the threshold when she anxiously asked him," How did it go? Judging from your exuberant mood I should say things went just as you expected."

"Mother dear, you're so right,"Tonio answered jubilantly. He hugged and kissed his mother, and both shared the good fortune that had come their way.

I knew that the Sibyl's fortune would come true. That's wonderful. Now, tell me more. What was the reaction of Prince Salinas, his son Phillip, and, of the other dignitaries there?"

"Mother, I'll tell you all about it after I've taken a nap. Believe me, I'm pooped," he answered yawning.

"Of course, son. Take a long rest. You'll need it to face your grandmother. And be alert. Don't risk life or limb on the rotten steps of her staircase.

That old bitch, queen mother of that salty wet-bottomed nation that inhabits the Striscia, wants to see you whether you want to see her or not… it's immaterial. The Striscia's ruler has spoken. I could just puke on her! Anyway, it's about a very important matter and it concerns you. The old bag kept the telephone ringing every fifteen minutes for the entire night asking whether you had returned home. She threatened that she would come here if you failed to see her first thing in the morning. Go to bed, my son, so that you'll be able to go see her. I don't want her to come here. If she did I'd kill her with my own hands," Elvira said with emphasis, strangling the air in front of her.

"Mother, do you really think I should go? I haven't been to see her in ages," Tonio asked, evidently reluctant to go.

"I bet she hasn't had those falling steps of her staircase repaired yet."

"She hasn't. With all her money she could have had those steps made out of pure gold. Instead she continues amassing all those riches, and lives like a destitute and eats her own shit."

"Mother, I rarely have ever heard you use such language."

"It befits that old bitch. She never offers to help us at all, even though we could clearly use it!"

"Did she give you any hint of what this is all about? Why she wants to see me immediately."

"Of course not. It's another one of her shitty secrets. I hope she's not interfering with our plans. You should go and find out exactly what she's up to."

"I'll go as you wish me to, mother, if I only knew whether she had those steps of hers fixed. I don't want to break my neck. Do you think she has?"

"I don't think so. In fact your father was, the last victim of their disrepair. Last Tuesday he went to kiss, the hand and to worship the wrinkled ass of that old bag, one of the steps gave in and he almost lost his left leg. I suggest you ask her to throw you a rope from the window and you can use it like an acrobat. A real Tarzan. It's safer that way," Elvira added sarcastically.

"Now, go to bed! I'll do the same."

"Good-night mother."

"Good-night son. I'll wake you up in time for the pilgrimage to the Striscia. Sleep tightly."

Very soon the lights went out in the Giaccone residence as Elvira proudly called the modest stucco house.

Chapter XI

Tonio, the next day went to see grandmother, but at sunset. In front of her gate he wavered, not having yet decided whether to go through with it.

"For one thing she's going to kill me for showing up so late. 'Better late than never' I'll tell the old lady. On second thought, why should I give her any explanation? I'd better call it off. No, wait. Once I've gotten this far I had better go up and slay the dragon," he concluded approaching the notorious staircase of the immense two story building of hard stone but visibly dilapidated from lack of upkeep. It was similar in design to his parents' house, but much larger.

The building's first floor was used as office space. The second floor was his grandmother's home. The old lady was left a widow when she was still a young and attractive woman. In order to avoid the slightest suspicion of any sentimental relationship between herself and her dark, handsome, and young accountant, Leo Martini, whom she had hired to manage her growing estate, grandmother had the first floor accesses to the second floor filled with stone and mortar. Thus, the second floor was made accessible only by the external staircase, which had been in need of an overhaul for a decade or more. Elvira had warned her son that until a week ago those steps were still broken. Great was Tonio's surprise when he saw the legendary risky steps finally repaired. The mason had just finished repairing them a short while before Tonio came and the cement was still drying. Wooden boards covered the steps protectively. Tonio lifted one board to see whether the old miser had made use of the old tiles. He saw that the steps were entirely remade of cement and bare of tiles. The old miser had cut corners again.

"Grandmother's such an old fool!" he cried. By chance his grandmother came out onto the balcony at that very moment and caught Tonio with the board still in his hand.

"Professor, put it down! You damn fool you!" she shouted. "Don't you see that those boards serve a purpose? Babies know that but professors don't. Do you know why they lay on top of the freshly finished steps? Because the cement's still soft. It isn't yet as hard as your marble head. Do me another favor and don't stand on that step any longer or you will lower it by a foot. Do I have to tell you everything? I bet these things are not in the books you read. You'll be surprised to know how many things there are to be learned besides Greek and Latin. How long did it take you to learn those trifles? Two decades? You have a fine mind, indeed. You and your presumptuous mother are two of a kind. Are you coming up or not? Make up your mind! Don't stand there like a fool," she said contemptuously and went in.

Tonio had a mind to retreat rather than go upstairs and be abused a lot more by that awful tongue. He took courage and climbed the wet steps. Concetta, the old maid, came to open the door for him. She was the same age as grandmother but, deprived of any intellect, she had escaped the cares which turn every thinking person into a precocious old age. She was round and ruddy like a girl. Mutely, like a fish, she guided Tonio into the living-room, decorated au fin du siecle. There reigned a great silence. The loquacious old bitch of a minute ago had turned into stone. She was sitting facing the half open balcony-door in an armchair as if it were a throne, and wearing a simple tunic of brown silk which covered her from neck to ankles and so adhered to her skinny and fragile figure that she appeared as a hieratic Egyptian Queen of the Old Empire. Her long white hair was pulled back and tied into a toup that left the regular features of her face with cheekbones slightly marked, completely exposed—all wrinkles, and old age spots, seeking refuge in the dim light that filtered in from the lowered venetian-blinds. Her brown eyes were as shiningly searching and subjugating as her tongue was sharply destructive. Those eyes were the epitome of her character of steel and of her pitiless soul. Tonio entered the room quietly and the old lady totally ignored his presence. She continued staring at the slices of sunset red light which came through the venetian-blinds. Tonio went to her and kissed her wrinkled right cheek. She pointed to a chair next to her and Tonio went to sit in it. For a few minutes the only sound heard in the room was the tick-tock of the old pendulum clock. Then abruptly, without, addressing herself to Tonio, in a sort of soliloquy, she began to say in a soft tone,

"I have waited for you for the last four days. You don't stoop to come here anymore. This house and I are not good enough for you. You only frequent aristocratic palaces, and villas, and you only kiss the hands and derrieres of princesses."

Then she sped up her tempo and stepped up the tone of her voice. "Only a cretin could have failed to notice that the princess would let him do all that hand and derriere kissing at a price."

"Grandmother, I don't understand all this."

"I am not surprised. As usual you don't understand anything. However, from the moment I came to know that Marietta Burruni was involved in it, I pumped it out of her, for a few lire of course, what exactly the aristocratic stiffs planned to do to you. I have tried to warn you so you wouldn't be taken in by them, and be humiliated. Why did you come here now after there is little or nothing left for me to do? Why did your father fail to grab you by the shoulder and drag you here in time? Didn't my son Gaspare tell you that I wanted to see you urgently?"

"No, grandmother. Besides, I didn't know that you wanted to see me until early this morning, when I got back home and my mother told me."

"And you show up here at sunset? Don't you have any respect for me, you damn fool?"

"I'm sorry, grandmother. I had previous engagements to attend, but did you say that Marietta Burruni was involved in something? Grandmother, please, can you be explicit for once?"

"I thought that as soon as I mentioned the name Marietta Burruni that you would be able to disentangle the skein by yourself. Not a chance in a million. You have such a thick head. After your mother you are the other heavy cross that God put on my poor son Gaspare's shoulders."

"I still don't get it."

"Must I tell you that Princess Salinas and Baron Amadeo took you in? Lord, thy will be done! I didn't think you were so thick in the head.

Your case is worse than I thought. Let me see if I can simplify things to such a point that even you can grasp them," she mocked him.

Tonio was red with rage.

"How much more of these abuses can I take before I go nuts and strangle this old bag?" he asked himself.

"Tell me," she continued, "on Saint John's day did you go down into the grotto and did you ask the Sibyl about who was going to be your future wife?"

"Yes, grandmother, I did." Tonio admitted blushing.

"Then it's true that you are a fine specimen of stupidity. Who on earth ever heard of a professor doing such a thing? Evidently my son Gaspare wasted all that money trying to give you an education. It's clear that you learned nothing, not even that the Sibyl's oracles are believed only by us ignorant folks and not by learned professors, especially those of your caliber," she said with a grimace of disgust on her face.

"Grandmother, please spare me your evaluations of my intelligence and of my knowledge and stick to the story," Tonio asked irritably. "You can't take it! It figures. Anyway, would you tell me who spoke for the Sibyl? 'A princess? A real princess? That's great'." grandmother asked him mockingly, and now having grown too excited to remain seated. She got up and began pacing the floor.

"Grandmother, how do you know all that? Who told you?" Tonio asked surprised.

"The Sibyl herself told me," she answered tartly.

"You mean Marietta Burruni?"

"By George, you got it! What perspicacity! What a third rate brain you have! That's my grandson all right. He only understands baby-talk. Now can you tell me who planned the oracle's words and who paid 5,000 lire to Marietta Burruni to shout them into your credulous ear?"

"You mean that Armando and Carlotta had it all planned for me? Why?" he asked, dawning on him that after all the old lady might be right in assuming that he had been taken in deeper than he had thought possible.

"Why?" he asked again.

"Because the princess wants to lay her hands on my money. That's, why."

"Grandmother, I don't mean to be disrespectful, but, I must tell you that you're wrong in your assumption that princess Salinas' love for me is a fake, and she is only scheming to get your money. She is not venial. Not that venial, I'm sure," he protested.

"You talk like a fool," the old lady replied.

"The princess has reluctantly agreed to marry you only for my money's sake, but she is not going to get it. She has forgotten that I've placed a preceding condition on my estate which she'll never see fulfilled. Anyway, my money alone wasn't enough of a price for her to stoop down to your level. She had to add a large slice of humiliation for you, too. You had to play the fool in front of her guests."

"Grandmother, that was before. Now she really loves me. Don't judge the princess too harshly, please, he pleaded.

"I can see that you're a born fool or that you'd like to play one forever. Put some common sense into your thick skull and marry a good girl from your own turf, also get my money, and live happily ever after."

"Grandmother, why do you insist on forcing Paluzza on me?"

"What's wrong with Paluzza? Isn't she a much better catch for you than a dissolute princess? Do you defend her because she gave you the 'privilege' of making love to her without wasting any time?"

"Do you know that, too? "Tonio asked bewildered. "She really is a witch," he thought.

"Yes, I do. Have you, ever thought on how many other men she has bestowed the same privilege?"

"It's immaterial to me."

"Well. Nonetheless, go and tell her that you

Passing the Torch

won't inherit a single penny from me and you'll see how fast she throws you out of her villa. Her villa! It's practically mine!" She went to a bureau, pulled out a drawer and drew out a file which she waved in front of Tonio's uncomprehending face. Look at these!" she commanded, exhibiting the file's contents: seven I O Us totaling a 10 billion and a half lire, and all seven signed by prince Guidelbert Salinas.

"These are all gambling debts that the prince can't pay off. And I have a lien on Villa Augusta, for them. Isn't that an extra incentive for the princess to get her claws into you? I should say so. Think about it, you numb-skull! What do you intend to do with her? For once in your life behave yourself like a man of honor! Now get out of here. Concetta! Concetta! She called aloud her servant.

Concetta came in running.

"Concetta, throw the professor out!" she commanded. "Goodbye, professor!"

"Grandmother, it isn't necessary to throw me out. I'll gladly leave, but first I have to ask you how come out of eight children and eighteen grandchildren, you chose me as your sole heir, and on the absurd precondition that I marry a fisherman's daughter!"

"Before answering your question I have to ask you one. Do you think I love you or do you suppose that I hate you? Answer me truthfully. Don't try to be a smart Aleck because I'd punish your insolence with a fat lip," grandmother warned him.

"Grandmother, I'll try to be as truthful as I can. Ever since I can remember you've always treated me unfairly…Now that I think of it, you treat everybody harshly."

"Harshly, eh! Go ahead."

"Grandmother you are really a very stern woman. You always treated me more harshly than your other grandchildren. Putting together all of the abuses and the rotten words and the smacks in the face you have piled on me through the years I'd have to conclude that you don't love me. But that would be a much too simplistic a deduction which certainly wouldn't begin to scratch the surface of your complex personality. You really love and hate me, and in an indeterminate and variable ratio between the two," Tonio answered. His analysis of her feeling toward him was actually a reflection of his own feelings for her.

"Professor, what's all this nonsense? Why don't you summon all your guts, they can't be too many, and tell me straightforward exactly that you think I hate you?" she taunted him.

"Alright then. I hate you as much as you hate me!" Tonio blurted out with a sigh of relief.

"Bravo! Do you know what you're good for? Nothing. Nothing absolutely! You can't make the distinction between the true love of a good girl and the play-acting of another, but, you can be so presumptuous as to analyze my feelings. I haven't sorted out my feelings toward you yet, and I haven't ever come to a clear conclusion, but perhaps you have hit the mark saying that I hate you. I must say it's hard for me to admit it, and, on the other hand, the truth is that I hate your stupid behavior, but I don't hate you. A twisted thought, I'm beginning to talk nonsense just like you. Anyway, my answer to your question is that I made you my sole heir because I wish to see you crushed under the heavy burden of my riches. They might not kill you literally and outright by their sheer weight, but by the constant thought they require, either to keep them or to increase them, and even to dispose of them. They'll send you to an early grave. In the final analysis I wanted to spare my other children the burden and put it entirely on your shoulders. My children and grandchildren already have enough troubles with what they possess now. In conclusion, my action was taken because, as you guessed it, I hate you. Now get out of here. Concetta! Concetta! See the professor to the door. Open it wide, and kick him out! Kick him so hard that he'll land on the ground skipping the still wet steps!"

Once again the two of them parted as unceremoniously as they had done in the past.

Tonio, kicked out of his grandmother's house

like a stray dog, mulled over the wicked old lady's words on his way home. She had planted in him the seed of distrust.

"How can I trust Carlotta from now on?" he asked himself. Was she truthful at the beach or was her declared love for me another proof of her acting abilities? I don't really know. I still love her but I can't take whatever she does or says at their face value anymore. From now on my mind and my ears will be open to doubt, in search of finding my loved one guilty of anything. Grandmother's skillfully turned me into a monster. Her revelations have succeeded in poisoning my love for Carlotta. Somehow I don't feel the same longing to see her. I'll go back to Villa Augusta this evening but I feel something's broken inside of me. I shouldn't have gone to see the old bitch. She killed that wonderful sensation I had of being in love and being loved in return—for myself, as I am, for what I am. Grandmother, give me my illusions back, please! What did I care if Carlotta pretended to love me just to grab my grandmother's money as long as I didn't know it, I didn't want to know. If I didn't know I could have lived happily with my illusion of being loved by the woman I really loved, and for the rest of my days. Now I've not only lost her love, but, also, the illusion of her love. I'll go back to Villa Augusta as her investigator rather than as her lover. It would have been better if I could go on as a fool but a happy one!"

Two hours later Tonio, was again at Villa Augusta, a guest of princess Carlotta Salinas. The villa was entirely lit and glittering, decked up for another party. Prince Guidelbert, his son Phillip, and Carlotta welcomed their guests with the requisite formality but also with warm friendliness. Carlotta introduced Tonio to her father and her brother. They treated Tonio as if he were the heir to the throne, Prince Umberto di Savoia, rather than the son of a fisherman.

"Are they fussing on me because they want to use me to retrieve the prince's I O Us from my grandmother's hands?" he thought. No sooner had this brutal thought emerged from his subconsciousness than he felt ashamed of having even thought of it and tried to erase it from his mind. He tried to enjoy himself as if he knew nothing of the schemes and falsehoods that surrounded him. Carlotta behaved as if she were really in love with him. She introduced Tonio to her friends, all titled aristocrats, of course.

"Here everybody's either a prince or a princess, a duke or a duchess, a baron or a baroness, just as at the Striscia, where everybody's a sea-captain," Tonio mused. "I'm not a sea-captain and

I haven't made cavalier yet. I guess I don't belong to either group."

Although none of the guests seemed to have noticed his lack of rank, Tonio suspected they tolerated him in their circle as a favor to Prince and Princess Salinas. In order to chase his awful thoughts away, he took Carlotta by the hand and led her to the center of the ball-room full of dancing couples. He asked the orchestra leader to play the lovely Tango del Mare. As soon as the orchestra began to play he put his arm around Carlotta's waist, pulled her warm body, wrapped in a green decollete of peau de soie, close to his body and they began to dance cheek to cheek. He felt so happy.

"Curse that old lady for wanting to destroy these enchantments," he thought. His jolly mood was short-lived, though, as he soon relapsed into the gloom of suspicion.

"Why have I chosen this tune 'Tango of the Sea' if not to vent my hostility toward Carlotta! I'm trying to distance myself, a fisherman's son, from her, a princess. I'm shouting: play a tune of the sea for one who comes from the Striscia. As if they didn't know that already. Cursed be she who put these atrocious ideas into my mind!"

No matter how hard he tried Tonio couldn't really enjoy himself. The worst came when at a discreet hour Carlotta led him into an ornate bedroom where they made love. Tonio found that the ecstasy of the night before wasn't there. The suspicion he had that Carlotta wasn't really in love with him spoiled his pleasure and poisoned the spring of their relationship. Somehow everything had gone flat and tasteless. He seemed to have detected bits of cold and artificial responses in her, even in their sensual intimacy. If she pretended having reached sublime ecstasy he pretended likewise. He too had become an impostor and a liar.

"Can this already dead love be revived?" Tonio asked himself, knowing well that that miracle would never happen.

Tonio returned every evening for a whole month, to see and love Carlotta, and every night he witnessed the dreadful erosion of their love and its approaching end. He tried to put the blame for this disaster on other people, on the environment, and even on the bedroom.

"The damn thing's too ornate, too distracting!" he complained. He didn't want to face the truth that his love for Carlotta was now dead and buried. As his burning passion had quickly turned into cinders, Tonio's visits to Villa Augusta became fewer and far in between. Carlotta saw Tonio's change of heart and tried to rekindle his love by catering to his slightest wishes. To no avail. She saw him slipping away from her just the same.

"The clod wants to go back to having his usual lentil-soup. The slob is sated with caviar," she commented in a rage.

On the other hand Tonio's problem was how to break off with Carlotta without hurting her feelings. At first he began skipping days, and now he was skipping weeks between his visits to Villa Augusta. Even then, Carlotta had to coax him for a promise he'd come back to see her. If the nobility hadn't lost that much ground she would have him hanged for such an impertinence. To make things worse her humiliations before him didn't even pay off. The end of their relationship came anyway.

The last encounter between them was painful for Tonio. That last night he had to spend with Carlotta seemed to him interminable. When it was time for him to leave her bedroom he sighed with relief. Carlotta saw him to the main door. It was a gloomy and rainy night, and against his objections Carlotta went out on the perron's landing to see Tonio off and get into his old Fiat and drive off.

Tonio turned his head and saw her still standing against the balustrade of the landing, and waving at him under the rain. He felt guilty and ashamed, but couldn't mend his broken love for her.

"Goodbye, Princess Salinas!" he silently cried.

"I should have had the guts to tell her: "This is the end. I won't come back here anymore. I wish you all the luck in the world, and I also hope that you find another young man more suitable than I. I'm sorry that things didn't work out between us. Who is to take the blame for the failure of our romance? Probably it's nobody's fault. As we say at the Striscia: 'It wasn't in the cards.' Goodbye, again!"

Tonio rolled the window up as it was now pouring, and the wind was blowing the rain into the car. With his high-beams on, and with the windshield-wipers at high speed he couldn't see too far ahead only streaking rain and darkness.

"They should put some lights on this damn driveway!" he cursed, feeling as gloomy as the weather he was driving through.

"I'm a fickle, obtuse, sanctimonious ass!" he scolded himself.

"I always manage to inflict pain on myself and on others."

Tonio reached the gate and almost stepped on the accelerator, when he saw a person or something in the shape of a person jump in front of the car. He jammed the brakes and fortunately missed running the careless pedestrian over by a few inches. Tonio came quickly out of the car and, "Are you crazy?" he shouted angrily at the fool ready to submerge him under an avalanche of profanities. His words died in his mouth when he found himself in front of Paluzza Oliveri. She stood there soaking wet, but defiant. She had followed him to Villa Augusta and had waited for him in front of the gate until he had come out.

"Christ, you almost got yourself killed! Are you totally nuts? What do you want from me?" he shouted at her irritably.

"You know exactly what I want from you. Don't you dare get involved with another woman. Do you have a mind to marry princess Carlotta Salinas? Don't. You won't marry anyone but me. The second your mother or the prince announces your engagement I'll kill you with this revolver," she said patting her raincoat pocket where a bulge revealed she kept it.

"I'm not marrying Princess Salinas. I don't even plan to see her ever again. Go home! Where is your car?"

"I took a taxi."

"Get in my car, then. I'll take you home."

"No, thanks. I'll hail a cab, but don't forget my threats you're mine or you're dead. Wait. Are you telling me the truth that you won't see Princess Carlotta again?"

"Swear it. And if I ever catch any hanky-panky going on with her I'll kill you! Do you hear me?"

"I heard you very well, and it's all right with me. Now go home or you'll catch pneumonia!"

"The bastard talks as if he cared," she whispered under her breath.

Tonio got back into the car and dropped her off at the portico of the Villa where a middle aged servant waited, hearing the screeching of the brakes and been sent to the car to inquire of the problem, he directed that a cab be summoned for the lady. The rest of his drive home was uneventful.

Chapter XII

"What caused its failure? Who caused it?" Prince Salinas was asking out loud for the hundredth time, leading his two, children and Armando into his study, down the corridor. They reached the study's door and entered. They all took seats at the three-legged card-table.

"What caused our plans to fail then?" the Prince asked once more. A deep silence followed. Armando tried to dispel the gloomy atmosphere by saying with tongue in cheek,

"As long as we're all sitting here at this tripod, why don't; we hold a seance and ask the dead to communicate to us what caused our plan to collapse?"

"Shut up, you fool!" the Prince rebuked him. "This is no time for your stupid jokes!"

Silence reigned again in the study. Then Armando broke it again.

"It cost me! It cost me five thousand lire! I gave Marietta Burruni five thousand lire! A lot of money for one in my financial distress. Cursed be the Sibyl!" he cried.

"It cost each of us a great deal in one way or another," the Prince sighed resignedly. It cost Carlotta more than money," he added broken-hearted.

Carlotta couldn't take anymore of this kind of talk. She left the study and ran to the veranda to be alone. She didn't want to burst into tears in front of the three men. Tonio had hurt her deeply. She had suffered the worst humiliation of her life. She leaned against the veranda's balustrade and began to think of a plan of revenge. He had hurt her as a Princess and as a woman. As a Princess she resented having been jilted by a fisherman's son, and as a young and beautiful woman who, in the past had initiated and broken off her relationships as she pleased, now she was the victim. He had dropped, her.

"The gall of a fishmonger daring to do that to me. I'll make him pay dearly for such an affront!" she vowed angrily.

Carlotta wracked her brains for a feasible plan of revenge. She couldn't come up with any short of hiring a hit man. That was out of the question. As there hadn't yet been any official engagement between her and Tonio, it would have been inappropriate to challenge him before a court of law or of honor. After a while she headed back to the study hoping that either her father or her brother or Armando had come up with effective plans. Instead, as she had suspected, the three cretins had spent the time arguing and piling, insults on each other. She was ready to leave the stupid scene of internecine conflict when she heard, Armando saying, "Tonio will be killed anyway by Paluzza Oliveri sooner or later. I bet on it," he reiterated.

"Paluzza vowed to kill Tonio if he ever got involved with another woman. The other night, when Tonio left Villa Augusta in the rains, Paluzza stopped him in front of the gate. She'd have killed him then and there if he hadn't told her he didn't plan to marry you, Princess, for added assurance just to save his own skin. He also swore that he didn't intend to ever see you again. Ergo, if we could find a girl who looks, like you, Princess, to be mistaken for you and if we also managed to put out our bait and Tonio on a rendezvous, and let Paluzza find them, I am sure she would kill him. You, Princess, could have your revenge without laying a finger on him," Armando told Carlotta and expected the Prince to second it.

"That will never happen," the Prince disagreed. Women like Paluzza always make those threats. Words alone don't kill."

"Prince, how is it that you never approve of my ideas?" Armando asked hurt.

"Because I've had more than enough of them. These brilliant ideas of yours are not pearls. The Sibyl scheme was the last gem that fertile brain of yours produced. Who else could have thought of it but a jerk like you!" the prince said, shaking his head.

Armando's idea struck Carlotta as capable of being put to use. She thought it could succeed if only she herself participated in the scheme rather than a look-alike who would be hard to find, after all, and if found, would need much convincing to play her part. Carlotta excused herself and went to her room. There she thought how to make the plan smooth and, practical. After a while she went, to bed still hammering the remaining flaws plaguing the plan. Finally she had every detail worked out to a pleasing state and let herself fall asleep at 4:00 A.M.

The following morning around 9:00 A.M., she called Turri Sicorene.

Turrio jumped with joy when he heard the sound of Carlotta's voice.

He had waited to be called for three months, and, by now he despaired, of hearing from her ever again. No sooner had princess Carlotta invited him to come to see her, as usual secretly by the back gate, at ten o'clock at night than he accepted her invitation. Turri had heard rumors about Tonio Giaccone being Carlotta's lover and he harbored a great resentment against her for her fickle nature, but he still loved her enough to forgive her. He jumped at the opportunity to see

Carlotta again. He put the blame entirely, on Tonio for having come between Carlotta and himself. His feelings twisted his vision of reality. He saw Carlotta, as Tonio's innocent victim. Tonio was no longer, in his eyes, his good friend and professor, but a monster as hairy as King Kong and as beastly. Tonio had trapped the innocent princess.

Thank God, she's, free now. Tonio is out of her life. From now on he'd better stay away from Carlotta or I'll kill him," he promised to himself.

"I'll, be there on time, my love," Turri told the princess. "To tell the truth, I'm overjoyed that you called at last. It has been a long time. I thought, you had forgotten all about me, and your promise," he added.

"Turri, how on earth could you ever think that I could do a thing, like that? I haven't, for a moment left you out of my mind or my heart. I still treasure the lovely piece of damask wrapped around the beautiful rose you gave me the first night you came to see me!"

"Jesus! How did he dare to bring that, dirty and stinking piece of rag to me?" she thought with revulsion.

"Do you really keep that piece of damask cloth for my sake?" he inquired, touched by her loving gesture.

"Of course, I do. It's a treasure, and I'll never

part with it as long as I live," she lied to him. "I hope the dope will never ask to see that dirty piece of trash because, I threw it in the wastebasket the very night he gave it to me," she said to herself.

"Turri, you don't want it back?" she asked him feigning hurt feelings.

"Oh, no, I gave it to you for keeps. It's yours," he answered with emphasis.

"What a relief it is to hear you wanting me to keep it. I couldn't ever part with it. As a matter of fact, I hid it in a safe place where nobody can find it and steal it from me."

"I know what you mean. It has a great sentimental value for me also," he confessed.

"It's our bond of love. Anyway, come to see me tonight. I want to smother you with my kisses," she said trying not to burst into laughter. "I have to use this baby-talk with this little boy in order to use him for my scheme."

"Smothered by your kisses is the best way for me to die. Do it tonight."

"Tonight!" she said in a most coaxing tone.

"I'll see you tonight," Turri repeated and hung up. He walked to his mother and embraced her.

"You shouldn't go to Villa Augusta at the snapping of Carlotta's fingers!" Gemma warned Turri, who was ready to run to see Princess Salinas that very moment. "Don't you see now that she's using you, you little fool?"

"Mom, I see that, but it doesn't matter to me. She owns me body and soul although she hasn't bought me at any market place and no transaction can vouch my bondage. She didn't want to be my mistress as I didn't want to be her slave; and yet, I am her slave, whether she wants it, or not. I have neither pride nor shame left in me. I do perceive that the power that chained me to her didn't chain her to me. However that perception still doesn't lighten my chains. She's not to blame for my predicament. What could she have done if a mysterious force had tied her to a moron like me without her asking for it? Nothing. I am hers, but, she isn't mine. Mom, that's what you are telling me, isn't it? As if I didn't know. Anyway, I remain, her slave. I feel this helplessness with her only. The other millions of women leave me cold and only she makes me want to worship her. If you have been in love you know what I mean, Mom. I've got to run to church. I'll see you later!"

"Are you, running to church to ask God to sanction your folly?"

"To ask Him to take pity on me," Turri answered. He opened the front door and headed for the Cathedral two blocks away. He walked from Magenta Street to Victory Square, climbed the twelve steps in front of the Cathedral, and entered it through the small door in one panel of the double paneled main doors. At ten o'clock in the morning that Wednesday there were no services, therefore there was nobody in the church besides him. A deep silence reigned in there and the huge church seemed larger still in the semi-darkness. No candles were lit except two in the main apse's sanctuary on each side of the Eucharist. Turri traversed the atrium and went to cross himself before proceeding on the Northern nave. Beyond there he reached the baptistry where he himself was baptized as a baby. Turri proceeded toward the proscenia. As soon as he got there he fell on his knees on the chancel's steps and prayed to the Madonna. It was easy for him and he didn't feel he was committing blasphemy to unburden his sorrows or to thrust his hopes on the Madonna, this mother more understanding than all mothers. After the Hail Mary, Turri began telling Her, "I've come to thank you, Mother, for having heard my prayers. You've softened princess Carlotta Salinas' heart to call me. I'm eternally grateful to you, Holy Mother. You know that she means everything to me. I'll go back to Villa Augusta tonight. Mom says I shouldn't go. She knows that I go to see Carlotta by night like a thief to steal her kisses. I can't help it, Mother! Is it a sin in your eyes to love someone with whom one has fallen in love? I know. You tell me I should have fallen in love with someone compatible to my age, status, and the rest. But, was it up to me with whom I would in fall in love? You know better than that, Mother of Compassion. I didn't kindle this burning fire inside of me with my own hands. I can't put it out either. If I could I wouldn't let it destroy me the way it has.

Therefore, I've come to you once more for help. It won't be enough for me to hold Carlotta in my arms for tonight only. Holy Mother, have her open her heart and put in it a little love for me, so that she'll be mine for life. You know better than anyone else that I can't live without Carlotta's love. Therefore let me live, dearest Mother, by making her mine or change my feelings toward her, take her out of my system!" he implored crying out audibly.

The bent and white-haired Monsignor Mariano, by chance, crossed the transept. and caught most of Turri's prayer. He had known Turri since his birth.

"The boy's so conceited. He's in love with a princess, no less, and talks to the Madonna as if she were a servant," the old priest commented, proceeding toward the sacristy.

Chapter XIII

Turri opened the wrought iron gate and entered Villa Augusta's, luxuriant gardens.

"'I've set foot once again in the garden of Eden," he sighed with gladness. "I regret to have said to my mother that Carlotta hasn't been smitten by love as I have. Perhaps she is unwillingly tied to me as I am tied to her, It could be a case of complementary chemistry and she needs my elements and components as much as I need hers to live a happy life. Whatever it is I know that she's got it, and it draws me irresistibly to her in a sort of magnetic field. Therefore I can't find peace away from her. I'm here to give my poor heart a brief respite and feed my passion with the few crumbs from her hand." Tonio crossed the walk flanked, by tall palm-trees and headed for the veranda's staircase. Carlotta's voice, from behind a citronella bush, dissuaded him from going upstairs.

"Come over here," she whispered.

He went behind the bush and found her in

the darkness of the night and hugged her and kissed her lips voraciously.

"How wonderful it is for me to embrace you again, my dearest Carlotta," he told her joyfully. Her verbena scent was driving him crazy with passion. He wanted to hug and kiss her again and again. Carlotta stopped him. She took him by the hand and led him to a nearby wooden bench.

"There are a few things you should know about me so that you won't judge me too harshly," she began to say.

"I'll never judge you harshly or otherwise," he protested.

"You have a noble heart, my darling," she complimented him "and the remainder of an ass," she wanted to add. "Anyway, this is what you should know. A rumor might have reached your ear about me and Tonio Giaccone," she said and sighed to express her annoyance.

"As a matter of fact it has. He's your lover, isn't he?" he asked in anguish.

"Do you believe that? If you do, then that is the truth."

"Are you saying that's not true?" hoped Turri.

"I am saying, what is truth? Anyway, this is my case. My father, as it is well known, is a compulsive gambler. In the last few months he has lost more than a million and a half lire at the gambling table. Being short of cash he wrote a few I O Us to cover those losses. Somehow those notes ended up in Tonio's grandmother's hands. The Prince hasn't got the liquidity necessary to retrieve those notes. The old lady was satisfied to have a lien on this villa, but Tonio has had something else in mind on how to use those scraps of paper his grandmother's clutching in those wrinkled wicked old hands. If you were not Tonio's close friend I would tell you of the base use he has put them ."

"I'd appreciate it if you would tell me all about it. First, because since I heard the rumor of his involvement with you I've stopped calling him my friend, and, second, if he has slighted you in the least, then I'll see to it that he makes amends for it or I'll cut his heart into pieces!"

"The punk's got spunk," she thought.

"Turri, this is very comforting for me to have someone as brave as you on my side. However, I don't want you to harm Tonio on my account. Promise me that you won't harm him or I won't confide in you."

"I promise," Turri agreed reluctantly.

"Good. Now I can let you know that Tonio has tried to win my affections by using my father's debts as a means to break down my refusal. You think he's lovely inside and out, but, I know better, and I can't stand him!"

"I always suspected that behind his debonair facade was hidden a low down skunk," Turri fumed.

"Not only that, he has also found an ally in my own father by telling the prince that his grandmother would forfeit her lien on Villa Augusta if I consented to marry him," she sighed.

"The brute, blackmailing you!" Turri cried angrily.

"You said it. Besides, he's a liar. He has pestered me with the lie that he is the sole heir to his grandmother's fortune, and if I married him I would come into a lot of money," she added.

"The insolent pig's trying to, buy you, Princess!" Turri shouted in disbelief, "and, I thought he was, a decent guy. He's rotten to the core. It figures that he's also a liar."

"Oh, one of the worst. I wouldn't marry him for all the riches in the world. Then I found out that if I had sacrificed myself for my father's sake and had married that brute he wouldn't have gotten a cent from that: lurid transaction because his grandmother, the old witch made a condition that he has to marry a fisherman's daughter to inherit her fortune. I never liked the malicious professor, but when I found out that he had been lying to my father and to me, I forbade him to set foot in Villa Augusta again. He hasn't resigned himself to staying out of my sight, and he has been trying to see me again for weeks. He has pestered me to the point that he finally has extracted a promise that I would see him one last time. As I won't allow him to come here, we will meet at Mondello on Thursday between midnight and one o'clock. You ought to know that I was at the Southern corner of that beach and it was at about that hour when he first saw me and began pestering me!" she sighed again.

"My love, if you don't want to see the beast again, then don't go to Mondello! I'll see to it that he won't ever bother you again," Turri said firmly. "Even if I have to kill him."

"The little Saracen's so brave. So stupid, but, so brave."

"How proud I am to have an escort like you rushing, so courageously to my defense," she complimented him in a tone that it almost gave her away that she was teasing him. However, I won't permit you to spill any blood for me. I've thought of a better plan to get rid of Tonio. On the surface it looks bloodier than yours, but it isn't. I hate violence, in any form and shape," she said empathically.

"I know that, my love. You couldn't kill a fly," Turri agreed.

"God, couldn't he have used a less revolting cliche?" she thought disgusted.

"How true! Anyway, in order to succeed, my plan needs your cooperation. Its success will permit us to love each other undisturbed by Tonio. My plan would tie him forever to his ex-fiancee, what is her name? Pamela Oliva? Palm Olive," Carlotta feigned to mistake Paluzza's name.

"Paluzza, Oliveri, is her name" Turri corrected her.

"I thank you, my love. Do you know her? I hope you do for that's where you come in to help me out," she asked.

"Do I know Paluzza? Of course I do. I was broken-hearted when Tonio and she broke up. He should marry that poor girl instead of going around bothering you!" he cried.

"My plan will do just that, and they will live, happily together ever after." ("Over my dead body," she thought.) "Isn't it great?" she asked feigning she craved for that happy event to come true.

"Yes, that will be great, especially for Tonio. Otherwise Paluzza will kill him one of these days if he insists on bothering you or any other woman. If I don't kill him first, that is," Turri added.

"Don't talk like that! Never again talk of killing anyone, please! Promise me!" she implored, all the while wishing that the boy would slaughter not only Tonio, but also the entire damned lot of them down on the Striscia. "I promise," he uttered reluctantly, "but if he ever again tries to bother you, then."

"There is no need, if my plan works. Did you

say that Palmuzza will kill Tonio if she finds him in a tete-a-tete with me?" she asked.

"I am sure of that. I know Paluzza well and she won't hesitate to kill him after he has sworn never to see you again to her-but you don't plan to see him again, do you?" he asked anxiously.

"Yes, I do, but only to get rid of him once and for all. This is my plan I'll keep my promise to see him at Mondello Thursday between midnight and one o'clock. That late hour is perfect for my plan and we don't need any spectators to impede its denouement. You should go and tell Palinessa when and where to find me and Tonio together. That's all I ask you to do or me, my darling. You have to make sure that Pasolinessa shows up at Mondello at the right moment. Can you, do that for me?" she implored him.

"I can do that for you, but, Paluzza has a, loaded gun on her and she'll kill Tonio immediately if she finds him in your company in the middle of the night," he said confused.

"No, she won't. I'll count on it. She'll find him trying to kiss me or worse, but, the coward, at gun point, will plead for his dear life, and will ask her to marry him if she will only spare his life. The plan will work, believe me!" she said convincingly.

"But wouldn't it be better and safer to tell Paluzza of our plan?" Turri objected.

"No. If she knew she might not be a good

actress and Tonio would find out that it's only a play and wouldn't ask the dame to marry him. It's better if you don't tell her anything and she'll scare the hell out of Tonio!" she said, bursting into laughter.

"I'll do as you ask, my love, although I think it's a little risky," said Turri.

"It's the only way they will live happily ever after, and we, also, will live happily ever after," she assured Turri.

"Speaking of our happiness, shouldn't we go to your room now?" he asked imploringly.

"No, my darling. I have been so upset these past few days that I can't relax until I get rid of Tonio. Then we will enjoy ourselves again and forever. You understand how I feel, don't you my love?" she trapped him into agreeing with her.

"Sure, my love, I can wait," he answered resignedly.

"Then go home, have a good night's sleep and go talk to Panizza first thing tomorrow morning. Afterwards call me, please, to let me know if you think I can count on what's her name showing up at the right moment at Mondello!" she said. She kissed him on his lips and gently pushed him toward the gate.

No sooner had Turri disappeared into the darkness of the night than Carlotta was back in her room to dress herself in something more suitable for the party being given in her honor by the Prince and the Princess of Parma-Bourbon. She took her red-flame suit off and slipped into a lavender organdy Balenciaga gown.

Chapter XIV

It was getting dark. Tonio didn't bother to turn the lights on, thus the study was faintly illuminated by the last rays of the setting sun reflected through the window panes. The study's decoration showed Elvira's hand and taste. This was evident from the satin goldenrod drapes to the stylized floating on air-misty background of the Far East prints hanging on the walls; from the basalt bust of Nefertiti on the mantelpiece to the rosewood book-shelves; and from the Chinese vases full of freshly cut yellow roses and white carnations. Tonio was sitting at the mahogany desk in an armchair with worn out black Moroccan leather, the chair had belonged to Luigi Pirandello, the famous playwright. Elvira had paid a fortune for it, in the hope that it would transmit by some mysterious osmosis the genius and artistic qualities of its previous owner into Tonio by the mere, act of sitting on it.

"This I've got to see," said Tonio, when he first sat in the chair. He had sat in it on and off for nine years and he still hadn't been able to write a single line of a scene let alone a full play. What presently bothered him was the thought of what he was going to do with his life.

"So far I've been a disappointment to myself and a pain in the neck to everyone I've come in contact with. If I only could find a way to make it up," he thought. Thus absorbed, Tonio traced, revised, erased, and retraced again in his mind the course of his actions on the coordinates originating in his heart and extending beyond the roofs of Cuntuvi into infinity.

"Will I do it right, this time?" he asked himself. "So far I've been a cheat," he sighed. "I promised eternal love to Paluzza and then I dropped her as if she were a cross on my shoulder. There she goes," he cried on hearing Paluzza pacing the sidewalk on her constant vigil over him.

"By refusing to marry Paluzza, I've also managed to hurt her parents, my grandmother, and my father. Princess Carlotta Salinas was only my second victim and I hurt my trusted friend Turri Siccorene by taking Carlotta away from him. My mother will be completely heart-broken when she finds out that I've dropped the princess. What am I going to do to make it up to all of those dear ones that I've caused to suffer?" he asked himself anxiously. "The best thing for me to do is to marry Paluzza even though I don't love her. I'll get grandmother's inheritance and then I can pay pecuniary compensation as it need be to everyone I've hurt so deeply. But I won't give Paluzza one dime. After all she only wants me, stupid and penniless as I now am, and that's what she'll get. And I'll make a gift of half grandmother's immense fortune to Princess Carlotta Salinas. Her financial distress has spoiled her life. Carlotta will then be able to restore the ancient splendor of her family and she can then marry Turri if she so wishes. A quarter of the inheritance will go to my sweet mother. She could buy those masterpieces she's been longing for. Lastly, with the remaining quarter of the inheritance I'll buy jewelry and precious stones and I'll distribute them to every woman in town to thank the few unknown women, who in the streets or in public places, caught my imagination and let me forget, for even one moment, the pain and anguish of living. I'll send an extra-big amethyst to Princess Elisa Sarzana, now past her prime and still beautiful. She gave me her delicate-hand to kiss and with it a touch of the sublime that I've since searched to find in other women, when I was still just an adolescent and she the most beautiful lady in Europe."

While Tonio was thus ruminating the telephone rang. It was Carlotta.

"Tonio, darling, you haven't come to see me in ages. Why?" she asked in a most casual tone of voice.

"I haven't had the time. This is the busiest season for us teachers," he lied, blushing because school had been closed for over a week.

"Could you come to see me tonight at eight?" she implored him. "The little bastard will decline for sure," she thought, "just as I want him to."

"Princess, I am sorry to say I can't, I have a previous engagement for that hour," he said trying to sound regretful.

"Would you come to meet me then at the Mondello at the same spot where we first made love, say between midnight and one o'clock, then? Please say yes!" she besought him.

Tonio, hearing her sad tone didn't have the heart to refuse seeing her there at that hour. "I'll be there, Princess," he said reluctantly, thinking "How am I going to tell her that I don't love her anymore. I assumed she has already understood that. Besides, this encounter between her and me is a little premature. I can't tell her yet that I've decided to marry Paluzza and that I intend to give her half of my grandmother's inheritance. However, I'll keep my word to see Carlotta tonight."

At eleven o'clock Tonio got into his old Fiat and drove toward the Mondello. He arrived at the beach at midnight. He parked the car and walked on the sand to the spot he well remembered where Carlotta would meet him. She wasn't there yet. Tonio sat on the tiny sand dunes and played with the sand letting it slide off his hand and thinking of the time when as, a boy he used to come here and build sand castles. Tonight, he hadn't come to build anything but to bury the withered flower of his love for Carlotta. It wasn't a happy occasion for either of them. While he was reminiscing he heard light footsteps skim the sandy dunes' surface. He turned his head and recognized Carlotta's silhouette. She was coming toward him in the faint light of the distant lamp light. When she came closer to him he saw that she wasn't wearing casual clothes suitable for the beach. She wore a green chiffon gown, and her bare shoulders were wrapped in an ermine cape. She's coming here straight from the Opera," thought Tonio.

He didn't love Carlotta anymore but he hurried just the same to meet her. They kissed each other as two old friends and stood silent for a while. Then Tonio gallantly took his brown flannel coat off, spread it on the sand and lent her a hand to sit on it. He sat down next to her on the bare sand. A few feet away from them the sea seemed to be murmuring their regrets.

"I see that all is over between us," Carlotta said dejectedly.

"I am sorry, Princess, that our relationship ended like this. I didn't mean to hurt you," he told her apologetically.

"It's the Sibyl's fault," Carlotta commented sarcastically.

"No, Princess, it's entirely my fault," he admitted. "I hope that you will forgive me for the wrong I have done to you, if not now, at least some day in the future. I hurt you deeply, I know that, but it was unintentionally done. You must believe that," Tonio pleaded with Carlotta.

She turned her head toward the parking lot to see whether Paluzza was coming as she hoped Paluzza would do. She wasn't there yet. "Perhaps my father is right in saying that women like. Paluzza have only a big mouth and never act. It makes me wonder whether that stupid broad will show up," Carlotta ruminated anxiously to herself.

"I wish I could believe in you again," she told Tonio, "but how can I? I bet you told Paluzza you were sorry after you ditched her. I'm sure you'll tell your next, victim that you're, sorry for having jilted her just as you are telling me now-how sorry you are for having hurt me. The truth about you is that you don't believe in anything, and least of all, in love. Why do you keep mentioning it then? Because you are a compulsive liar in the same way as my father is a compulsive gambler," she told him bluntly. "I've to keep talking to fill the time until Paluzza shows up!" she ruminated. Then I have to throw myself into his arms, although it makes me sick just looking at his big stupid face, and, all to make Paluzza think she has caught us making love. With this low down bastard? Never again, sister! Even pretending doing it will make me sick to my stomach. You stupid bitch, just come and do your duty: Kill, him! Then do me another favor: Kill yourself too!" Carlotta took another look in the direction from where Paluzza should come and, she gave a sigh of relief. The bitch was coming, at last. "This was the time," Carlotta thought, "to clasp Tonio and to kiss him and somehow wrestle with him!" Tonio, taken completely by surprise by Carlotta's behavior, couldn't resist nor discourage her. Before he could disentangle himself from Carlotta's embrace and her fit of maddening passion, Tonio noticed that another shadow had been suddenly added to their two. He lifted his head and quickly recognized the familiar green overcoat and the yellow fichu of Paluzza.

"That bitch has followed me again!" was his first thought in dismay. In the faint light of the distant lamp lights, he also noticed that Paluzza had a revolver in her hand. He suddenly remembered her threat to kill him if she caught him with Carlotta, and here he was, in an apparent compromising situation with the same Carlotta he had sworn never to see again, and on this deserted corner of the beach.

"God! She'll kill me!" he thought. He freed himself from Carlotta and jumped to his feet and ran toward Paluzza. My love, don't shoot!" he pleaded. "It's not what you think. The Princess and I were saying farewell forever. I have decided to ask you to marry me. Will you, Paluzza?"

Paluzza didn't answer.

"I'm telling you the truth. Don't shoot me! Please!" he pleaded, walking very close to her. Paluzza, kept quiet and suddenly shot him five times.

"She killed, the bastard!" Carlotta, said to herself and ran toward the parking lot where she had parked her red Alfa-Romeo. Before she could reach the parking lot two robust men ran after her and grabbed her. They dragged her back near where Tonio and, Paluzza were. To her amazement Tonio was still alive. Not only that, but he wasn't bleeding. He just was standing there amazed and speechless by the turn of the events.

"Bring the Princess here close to me!" Paluzza ordered the two men.

At the sound of Paluzza's voice Tonio came alive.

"You're not Paluzza," he cried. "That's you, grandmother?" "That's, me," she answered taking, off her rubber mask. For crying out loud, will somebody tell me what's going on here?

I don't get it," Tonio said, frustrated.

"With your brain and your intuition what do you expect?" Grandmother commented disappointed, "Don't you understand that the Princess here conspired, to have you killed by Paluzza? She brought you here according to her criminal plans so that if I had been Paluzza here, you'd be dead by now. The bullets I fired at you, were blanks. Had Paluzza shot you with live ammunition you'd be quite dead by now," grandmother repeated emphatically.

"How did you learn about this plot to murder me?" Tonio asked.

"Your friend, Turri Sicorene, see what kind of friends you've got? To me just another idiotic boy, and the town is full of them, went to Paluzza and told her all about this planned encounter between the princess and you. They hoped that Paluzza, in a rage at seeing you and the princess together here at this hour of the night, wouldn't hesitate to kill you. Who wouldn't do that in her place? However, Paluzza isn't as dumb as the princess thinks. She sensed that something was fishy and the smart girl came to me for advice. I told her to leave it to me. Paluzza and I simply exchanged places, and here I am. You'd be dead by now if I hadn't foiled the Princess's plan, you know."

"Is this true, Princess?" Tonio asked Carlotta, hoping she would deny, it. She turned her head away.

"I know I hurt you and I did you a very great wrong and the way I told you. I told you how sorry I was, and I would make it up to you my giving you half my inheritance," he whispered into Carlotta's ear.

"What did you say?" Grandmother asked Tonio.

"Nothing, grandmother, I was talking loudly to myself, having realized that you've been right all along and that I am a fool, through and through," he sighed.

"So, what else is new? Now all of you, leave me alone with her majesty here," she ordered the men.

They deferentially retreated from the two women.

"Your highness, it's way past my bed-time and I'll try to be brief," the old lady began to say as soon as the men walked away.

"You've committed a terrible felony and my three lawyers whom, I've brought along, they're standing in the parking lot. You can spot them from here. Now I'll give you a choice, either to go to jail for a few years for your criminal action or to accept my benevolent deal and immediately leave the country, and leave somewhat richer."

"I won't deal with a witch like you," was the princess' answer.

"Go to jail, then. My grandson will press charges against you. I'll see to it," the old lady said meaning it.

Carlotta had second thoughts.

"What's in your deal?" she asked matching the old lady's cool attitude.

"It's all in this brief-case. Here, open it," she handed the brief-case to Carlotta. "You'll find your father's I O Us, a cashier's check for ten million lire, plus a quarter of a billion lire in cash. Whatever is in the brief-case is yours on one condition, which is, that you leave town and the country immediately, and without going back to Villa Augusta. It's a very good deal, isn't it? Take it, please, before I change my mind and call those lawyers, who are dying to see you go to jail. They can't stand anything towering above their mediocrity. Destroying you is for these sons of bitches, if you pardon my French, like storming the Bastille!" The old lady spoke these words more imploringly than menacingly to Carlotta.

The princess opened the brief-case, checked the I O Us, the check of a million lire, and counted a bundle of bills. They seemed to add up to a quarter of a million dollars. She closed the brief-case, clutched it under her arm, wrapped herself tightly in her ermine cape and left without a word. She got into her red Alfa Romeo and disappeared in the darkness of the night, followed by the two robust men in a Fiat 100, to make her stick to her promise to leave the country immediately. It was then that Grandmother had a talk with Tonio.

"Grandmother, where did you send Carlotta?"

"To Hell, where else. What a bitch-fox she is. She's got a first rate brain, though, while yours is third rate, if not lower, if we have to, call a spade a spade."

"Grandmother, leave me alone please!" Tonio cried resentfully.

"Has it taken the barrel of a gun pointed at your stupid head to bring you back to your senses. In a manner of speaking, that is, if we can attribute any sensitivity at all to inert fossils like you."

"You never stop denigrating me, do you?"

"Am I denigrating you? No. God knows I'm speaking the truth. In fact, it took a blast of dynamite into your granite head to open your eyes that Paluzza's the right wife for you. I hope that you meant it when you proposed to her. Did you?"

Grandmother was waiting for an affirmative answer from Tonio. He turned facing the sea but remained silent.

"Speak up boy! Let me hear the sound of your lovely voice, and do it quickly, before the chill of the night kills me." She said with sarcasm.

Turri wanted to retract the proposal of marriage he had made to Paluzza under duress. It was true that he had come to the conclusion that the best thing for him to do was to marry Paluzza in the circumstances that called for it until a few minutes ago. Now there was no reason to keep his word. Grandmother's own intervention had revealed Carlotta's plot to kill him had been foiled and also had set him free. There was no reason for him to marry Paluzza, in order to inherit grandmother's fortune and give half of it to Carlotta.

"Grandmother, I don't need your damn inheritance anymore-Give it to charity. Build a monument to Adam Smith, your patron saint. Give a few millions of your money to Paluzza, so she can marry a good young man of the Striscia I can't marry her. She'd be a hindrance to the realization of my plans."

"What plans?" she chided.

"Lofty plans." He answered.

"Such as?"

Grandmother, I can't be specific. It's an amorphous hankering, a secret pain, a wish to enter immortality by a creative effort that will last as long as or longer than the Pyramids."

"You're a shit of a man. You're trying to avoid the responsibilities of life by dreaming of glory in an ivory tower. And I'm telling you, there is more nobility of purpose in tilling the soil than in writing the Divine Commedia, King Lear, or composing Madame Butterfly! Foolish man! Foolish boy, to be precise!" He hasn't grown up at all, she mused.

"He still believes in the fairytales that his pompous high-brow mother tells him. One can argue that he wasn't too bright to begin with, but that pretentious broad of his mother stunted whatever modest wits nature had endowed him with," she left unsaid.

"Marry Paluzza!" she repeated. "It would better for your chances of happiness. She will take care of the house, the children, she'll manage the inheritance and what not. She'll take good care of you, of course. You need a lot of care, my boy! She'll set you free to do what you like, mainly reading. You can read all the damn books you care to read, and dream at will with your ass wide open."

"She doesn't understand the subtle cravings of the soul. I am sure she has heard a million times that man doesn't live on bread alone. That simple truth has escaped her little mercantile mind.

I'll marry Paluzza, only to please you, Grandmother." Tonio said as if those were the words of a dying man. Tonio was married to Paluzza two months later, in a decision that was the lesser of two evils. The alternative was suicide.

Grandmother Giaccone hailed it as the only rational decision her erratic grandson had ever made. On the other hand, Elvira thought it was the most irrational decision and the ultimate folly she had least expected from her son.

"It's all the product of that old bitch Giaccone's machination. The old bag has finally pulled one over me. It will take me to an early grave." Elvira muttered in church, sitting next to her archenemy, during the wedding ceremony.

"How can Tonio get married to a broad from the Striscia?" She kept repeating to herself in disbelief. Elvira had expunged the Striscia's inhabitants from the book of life, as the pits of humanity.

"Poor son of mine, what will become of you in company of creeps!" She uttered, sobbing and drying her tears with a white monogrammed handkerchief, before they dripped down her eyes and cheeks, and marred her make-up. Elvira piled the blame for this marriage on her husband, the spineless being sitting at her side who hadn't a single thought in his stupid mind, itching solely to get rid of his formal attire, especially of the ascot and the shoes. Elvira tried to forget her husband's clan of brutes, who filled the Cathedral. The stench of fish was so strong that the odor of incense burning couldn't abate it. Elvira concentrated her attention on her son. Tonio was kneeling on the altar's step, next to that stubborn little bitch, who would soon become her daughter-in-law. Elvira could only see the veiled head of

Paluzza and the nape of the familiar head of her son.

"Tonio, what a stupid head yours turned out to be!" She uttered, venting her disappointment. She held her composure to the end of the wedding ceremony to the point of congratulating the newly weds, but she broke down outside, on the Cathedral's steps, and began weeping profusely. Gemma di Motia came to comfort her. "Poor Elvira!" she cried compassionately.

"She's crying tears of joy." Grandmother Giaccone interjected, with a pinch of venom.

"Isn't it true, my dear Elvira?" the old bitch rubbed in, giggling with pleasure.

Elvira hardly resisted the temptation to slap the face of the wrinkled like a dry prune of her mother-in-law. She got into her limousine in a hurry, toward the Ambassador Hotel, where the reception was to be held. She didn't allow her husband to accompany her.

"You can share the old bitch's limousine!" she shouted at Gaspare, who was left standing on the sidewalk while the limousine with only his wife in it, sped away.

After the reception at the Ambassador, Elvira locked herself in her house. She refused to let her husband or Tonio come in. It took three months before she relented and allowed her son to come and see her.

"Mom, what's done is done. Try to accept it. Don't add to my unhappiness by clinging to the illusion that by marrying Paluzza, I sold out my talent. I thought likewise up to a few months ago. Can you stop and stay still for a minute listen to me?" he pleaded, sitting in an armchair in the living-room, while his mother was dashing about, in and out of the room, pretending to be dusting the furniture.

"Don't tell me that by marrying Paluzza you haven't given up your dreams of becoming somebody. Will she be pushing you up the ladder and beyond? Bah!"

"Mother, if I had any talent, even Paluzza couldn't stifle it. Listen to me. The talent you thought I had was like the mirage a thirsty traveler sees in the middle of a desert. You saw in me what you wanted to see, which wasn't there."

"You had it, and you blew it."

"Mom, don't you think I wished with all my heart that I really had it? Unfortunately it was an illusion we both shared. Many mothers believe their children are geniuses. But talent is a rare commodity. The crucible of life will tell who the fortunate ones are, who possess it. I don't have what it takes to be among the great. I'll always be a college professor and nothing more than that," he said dejectedly.

Elvira went to embrace her son and comfort

him. Both wept for a while, in each other's arms. They let their heated emotions cool down somewhat before going to sit next to each other on the blue Empire sofa. Tonio, just because your talent has been late to flourish, doesn't necessarily mean that you don't have any. I would say you're a late bloomer." Elvira said with a residue of hope.

"Mother, it's hopeless. I threw in the towel when I found out that Mondadori editors agreed to publish a collection of short stories by my former pupil, Turri Sicorene, on his first attempt, a few days before I'd got another rejection notice in the mail for my last novel and on my tenth attempt. It was really then and there that I decided to marry Paluzza. Up to that time, I believed I couldn't marry her because she'd sap my talent. When I realized that I hadn't any talent whatsoever, I didn't have anything to lose by marrying her, except my ridiculous pretentiousness."

Mother and son kept quiet for a while.

"Mom, the fact is that Paluzza and I deserve each other. We are two of a kind. Two numbskulls." Turri uttered the last words trying to sound nonchalant.

"So, you really think that Turri Sicorene has talent and you don't? I'm not sure of that. I think that that punk's had some luck, that's all. The truth is that in his entire puny body, he hasn't the talent that you have in your pinky."

"And yet, Mom, please let's not rob Turri of his talent and bestow it on me. It's settled. Let's talk about something else. Paluzza and I would greatly appreciate it if you'd come to our place for dinner tomorrow night. Paluzza has her faults, but she's an excellent cook. Will you come?" he pleaded.

"I'll come, but not tomorrow night. In the future- maybe. Give me a little more time," she pleaded in turn.

"I understand, mom. Whenever you're ready." Tonio said with great disappointment. Then he left. He had felt that his mother wanted to be left alone.

"She's making a Shakespearian tragedy out of the insignificant foundering of my literary ambition." Tonio ruminated on his way home. On the surface he had philosophically accepted the demise of his dream of fame, and yet, deep down, his heart was still aching over the failure.

Chapter XV

The clock on the Taxation Building-tower struck 7:30 A.M.

"How time flies away!" Gerald Nascone commented without any real regret of it, passing by. Time for him had meaning only in reference to the working hours, as, for instance, how long until the beginning of that daily servitude. When at work he was always watching the clock asking,"When will it be over, never?"

At the end of the day he thought in terms of how long until working time again. Gerald didn't have a cosmic perspective or a metaphysical insight on time. He could waste a lot of it just faking at work. Before and after working hours he wasted a lot of time either doing nothing or aggravating his neighbors. He usually went to work much earlier than his fellow-employees. Thus every morning he could indulge in chatting for a while with Joe Ferraci, the owner of the optical shop located next to the Taxation Building.

This morning as usual Joe was on the shop-threshold waiting for Gerald to show up. He spotted Gerald coming from the corner of Magenta Street and followed him with his eyes until he came a few feet closer to him. "Good morning, Gerald! You voracious pig! On the other hand how can I suppress calling a spade a spade when I see your drum-like belly?"

"Good morning to you, Joe. You're so thin. Do you eat your donkey's hay? You're good for a famine-poster or a death-warning."

"We're in for another scorching day," Gerald commented lifting his head toward the serene sky.

"You'll benefit from it by selling a lot of sunglasses. Good-luck to you!"

"I thank you, Gerald. Could I sell a pair to you? At a discount of course."

"No thanks. I don't have: any use for sunglasses. I toast myself in the shade."

"Here come the night-creatures!" Gerald cried noticing a group of barons and cavaliers coming out of the Bourbon Club. "They'll lose their shirts gambling all night at the club, while their wives lose their virtues at home in their absence! Here comes Prince Guidelbert Salinas, a cuckold of epic and national rank."

Prince Salinas sneezed. "Salute!" Gerald wished the prince. "When the rams sneeze it's a sign of good weather," he commented out loud.

Prince Salinas' face turned purple at the insult thrown at him. He broke away from the crowd and holding his walking cane at one fourth of its tip with its ebony head in striking position, walked toward Gerald. From his brisk and determined pace it was clear the prince was going to confront Gerald to avenge the insult thrown at him. Joe Ferraci retreated into his shop.

"Oh! The cuckold is looking for trouble!" Gerald thought alarmed. "If he dares strike at me with that cane I'll kick him yon know where and while he is shrieking and with pain on the pavement I'll cream him with his own cane," Gerald ruminated getting ready to meet the prince's challenge.

"I'll hit him first on his, stupid head," the prince thought, "and then I'll tell him that he's a, cuckold himself, thus spilling the beans after sixteen years of silence. He won't believe me, though."

The prince now was only five feet away from Gerald who stood very pale on the sidewalk braced for the challenge.

"I'll wind up in jail for sure, after committing this inevitable crime," Gerald thought. He heard the prince uttering something ominous.

"A menace before striking—," Gerald thought.

Instead the prince asked, "Mr. Nastone, have you a match?" getting a Macedonia from his golden cigarette-holder and sticking it between his lips.

"Sure, your highness. I'm at your service anytime." Gerald answered with a sigh of relief. He got a book of matches from his coat-pocket, struck one and lit the prince's cigarette.

"I thank you, Mr. Nascone, for your kindness. Good-bye," the prince said inhaling the lit Macedonia. He soon went to rejoin his friends. They walked all together and soon disappeared at the corner of Fiorino Street.

"Jesus! That was a close call for me," Gerald commented while the flow of his blood was returning to normal.

The morning was still young and Gerald's sparring wasn't over yet. Cavalier Alvaro Mezzapelle had turned the corner of Fiorino Street together with Prince Salinas and the others and had reappeared from Loggia Square.

"Here he comes, Cavalier Mezzapelle, the regional heavy-weight champion cuckold. Mrs. Wanda Mezzapelle is the most beautiful perverse blonde broad of the region. In my opinion cavalier Mezzapelle will keep his title for a long time, although the competition to dethrone him is very keen," Gerald laughed.

Cavalier Mezzapelle came near Gerald and greeted him good morning.

"Could I have a word with you, Mr. Nascone?" he asked in a gentle tone of voice.

"No." Gerald answered brusquely. "I don't talk to cuckolds."

"With your attitude toward cuckolds sooner or later you're condemned to talking to yourselves. Cuckoldry is a common disease around here, and is very catchy, like the common cold. It seems that you are the only one immune to it. Be grateful, and show compassion toward us poor victims. As a matter of fact I'm here to ask you for a little of your compassion. I'd appreciate it if you'd stop calling me a cuckold whenever and wherever we meet, please. After all, you and I do have something in common."

"Not horns."

"Not that I know of. You and I have daughters the same age. My Annabelle and your Ann are both sixteen years old and go to the same school."

"Unfortunately. I keep telling Ann to stay away from Annabelle."

"Oh! To avoid the contagion of moral corruption? It's your choice, although I can absolutely assure you, that Annabelle is every bit as pure as Ann."

"It's only your opinion, Cavalier Mezzapelle."

"It is the truth! And, it's because of my daughter's future that I'm here at your feet, Mr. Nascone!" the Cavalier implored and knelt beseeching Gerald.

"Cavalier, please get up! Don't embarrass me in public!" Gerald asked helping the cavalier to his feet.

"Good for me that I changed my socks this morning," he joked.

"I thank you for your kindness and I'm begging you to restrain your impulses as moral crusader toward my wife and me. After all, we are all sinners as Saint Paul says. My wife and I aren't exceptions. We haven't done you harm. Therefore, please try not to call me a cuckold in public or you'll compromise my daughter's future now that it's time for a young man of our rank to set his eyes on Annabelle, and who knows, propose marriage to her. I'm asking you to close one eye on my wife's infidelities as I do."

"Sir, instead of coming here and asking me to stop calling you a cuckold you should ask your wife to remember she has a sixteen year old daughter, and to stop entertaining lovers for her daughter's sake. Good-day, Cavalier Mezzapelle! It's eight thirty and I have to go and earn my daily bread by the sweat of my brow. Not all of us can afford to do nothing like you rich Cavaliers." Gerald uttered in a tone of mixed, rage and sarcasm, and disappeared behind the huge green door of the Taxation Building.

Cavalier Mezzapelle lingered on the sidewalk a few seconds dejected, and also surprised at Gerald's crude behavior.

"I wasted my breath trying to turn a sanctimonious ass into a civilized human being," the Cavalier mused and headed toward home.

The moment he disappeared, Gerald came running out the door looking for him. "Too late." Gerald had realized he'd been too harsh on the cavalier and wanted to apologize, to tell him that he'd try to keep his tongue in check. In the meantime Joe Ferraci had come out of his shop.

"Gerald, have I witnessed seeing the lion and the lamb lie together? Wasn't it Cavalier Alvaro, Mezzapelle I saw conversing with you a minute ago?"

"Yes, you saw us together, but there's no peace on earth yet. He's not a bad guy, though. The Cavalier could have avoided being made a cuckold by doing the same thing that I did."

"What did you do?"

"I married an ugly woman. Boy is Paolina ugly! No man in his right mind would ever try to seduce her. I myself get close to her only when it's very dark and stormy, and I get so loaded that I know or feel nothing!"

"Gerald, you like to exaggerate, don't you? I bet Paolina has an ugly veneer but that she's dulcis in fundo."

"What's that Latin?"

"Gerald, don't tell me you don't know Latin."

"No, I don't know Latin. I've no use for it.

Now that you know that I don't know Latin and also that I've got an ugly wife, can we go on being friends as before?"

"Gerald, don't be silly. Of course I value your friendship. Nothing's changed between us."

"Joe, you can afford to be magnanimous because you know every thing and I bet you have a beautiful wife. Is she extraordinarily beautiful?"

"In my eyes Vera is the most beautiful woman on earth."

"Good for you! But, if your wife is so beautiful isn't there a chance that you're a cavalier without knowing it?"

"No, I am not. The truth is you're envious. Why then didn't you marry a beautiful woman?"

"I don't envy you for having a beautiful wife because I did deliberately marry the most plain woman. When I was a very young man I promised myself that I wouldn't become a cuckold. I didn't want to be one of the herd of rams roaming over this island."

"Being made a cuckold isn't the end of the world, is it?"

"It is for me! Therefore, I married Paolina. Shall I describe her to you?"

"No, please, I just had my cappuccino. However, in your case, wouldn't it have been better for you to be married to a beautiful woman and drink the elixir of the gods rather than drinking poison day in and day out?"

"Joe, you're wrong again. Like Rasputin, I've gotten used to taking in poison and I've survived. On the other hand, the knowledge of my wife being unfaithful would have killed me instantly. My mind's at rest while yours is constantly wondering what your beautiful wife is doing and with whom. Do you suspect her of any wrongdoing?"

"No! Vera is a saint!"

"Maybe when the sea is calm, but in a tempest? Unfortunately the seas that any beautiful woman has to cross are often in tempest and rarely calm. She finds many treacherous reefs trying to shipwreck her modesty. If I were you I wouldn't let Vera spend her vacations at Sferracavallo all by herself."

"Vera isn't by herself there. She's sharing a cottage with her sister, Margaret."

"Oh! Come on, Joe! You're kidding me! You're always complaining what a whore Margaret is and now you're telling me that you trust her to safeguard your wife? If I were you I wouldn't spend the summer here all by myself."

"Someone has to stay here and work to keep the ship afloat!"

"And where are your children? "

"They're at the Viscione with my mother. They usually spend the summer there."

"While your wife spends it at Sferracavallo sunbathing and swimming, and frolicking about in a skimpy bikini like any unattached girl. For a beautiful woman it's too risky to be alone among so many hungry men in a summer resort. Aren't you afraid she might be unfaithful to you? The odds are against you, Joe!"

"I know that, but since our wedding-day I've trusted Vera and she me. It's been well worth the risk of her being unfaithful to me than depriving myself of all the joy she's given me. Have a good day, Gerald!" Joe said reentering his shop.

Gerald lingered for a while outside. "How long can I go on being a liar?" he asked himself.

"I've told everyone I don't care about not knowing Latin or all the other knowledge I didn't get because my parents couldn't afford to keep me in school past 8th grade. The biggest lie of them all is that I deliberately married my ugly Paolina to avoid being made a cuckold. The truth is that I'd rather have married the beautiful Amalia Montalto and would have gladly taken the risk of her being unfaithful than basking in Paolina's secure reservation. A day spent with Amalia would have been better for me than a century with Paolina. I'd have been happier if I'd been allowed to hold Amalia in my arms even one day on leap-years than dying of regret a little each day. Amalia's parents had to break up our romance because I was below their status and they married her off to Carlo Buzzuni, the rich lawyer. Will I go to my grave playing the clown while my heart is actually bleeding? It's 8:30 A.M. Time for me to get in there and immerse myself in my work and try to forget my secret pain."

Chapter XVI

"When I was a boy this street and all those buildings weren't there. From under our feet to those rocks that was all there was, all sea then. In the last twenty-five years the bay has been filled up with debris from the demolition of the old Villa Franca castle and ramparts. The shore line was where those palm-trees now stand. My parents' four room house stood exactly where that gray high-rise building is. My house, as you can see, is now gone together with other places full of my childhood memories. I think I've told you before that I was born here on the Striscia."

"Dad, you've told me that a thousand times or more."

"Don't be a wiseguy! A thousand times he says! Even if I had told you a million times what kind of respect are you paying to your father talking like that? Couldn't you have listened to it one more time without shitting on me, you brat? You forget that I'm your father."

"Cool down, dad. I didn't, mean it."

"Then watch what you say. Anyway, do you ever come here?"

"No. Why should I?"

"Is the Striscia beneath you? You only frequent the mansions, and the palaces up on the hill. You mingle only with the rich and the powerful and you haven't finished the Liceo yet. I can imagine what a pompous ass you'll be after you go to the university and become a lawyer. Anyway, I come here often because as I was telling you I was born here, just right under where you're standing now. I could say I was born under your feet, thinking of it. Since I can remember I've always been under someone's feet. What a life! Have I told you before that my father was a poor fisherman who went fishing in a boat no larger than a nutshell?"

"Dad, no more of this crap, please!"

"Another crack like that and I'll smack you right in your stupid mouth. John, are you paying attention to me?" Gerald asked his son who had his mind elsewhere.

"Of course, Dad."

"Now I see that you're interested only in watching the derriere of every young woman passing by."

"Dad, I'm listening to you, honest, I am."

"Open your ears, then. Does honor mean anything to you?"

"It means a lot to me."

"Does it? How come you're so careless with it then?"

"Dad, I safeguard my honor with my own life."

"If that were true of you, you wouldn't drag Prince Phillip Salinas into our home knowing what a womanizer he is. Don't tell me that you don't know that Phillip has seduced all the young sisters of your other schoolmates!"

"Of course I know that, but what has it got to do with us? There aren't any girls at our house to tempt him."

"Christ! What do you think your sister Ann is, a piece of furniture? She's sixteen years old already!"

"Dad, don't make me laugh! Ann is a scrawny little kid. Phillip, has a million women at his feet, all as lovely as Venus, while my sister wouldn't attract the attention of a sailor ashore after six months out to sea. I love my sister, but she's no beauty. Besides, mother dresses her up in these awful clothes.

"Jesus! Besides being stupid, are you, also blind? Haven't you noticed that Phillip has already, how shall I put it politely? *Touched* her? Your mother noticed, how he, little by little, approached Ann while you thoughtlessly stared at the sky."

"I don't believe it. It can't be true!"

"It's true, you goddamn fool! Your mother grabbed your stupid sister by her neck and made her confess. She admitted she loves Phillip, your friend. What a friend! The stupid little broad doesn't know anything else but she knows that. She's in love. What do you know, even stones harbor passions."

"Dad, it's hard for me to swallow this improbable love story. I haven't noticed anything. Phillip comes home with me twice a week for a few hours so that we can study together. I don't see anything wrong in that. I go to Villa Augusta myself a couple of days each week to study with Phillip there. So we alternate sites. Do I have an ulterior motive for going there to seduce his sister Carlotta, for instance?"

"Princess Carlotta might try to seduce you is more likely. I hear stories about her "licentiousness" which just go to bear out my low opinion of her and the whole lot of them. Promiscuity is a way of life for them. Hers, has she given you the baptism of fire yet?"

"Dad, you don't know what you're talking about!"

"Is yours a case of real naivete or gentlemanly behavior? And so the circle of this island is completed."